Sugarland

By

Jo Dee

Aquarri

Sugarland

ISBN 13: 978-0-9914356-0-9

ISBN 10: 0991435605

Printed in the U.S.A.

For Tasha

Succubus: a female demon or supernatural entity that appears in dreams, who takes the form of a human woman in order to seduce men, usually through sexual acutivity...

She exists!

Prologue

Originally there were seven names! Seven names burned into her brain, seared into her thoughts, seven words of foulness merged with her soul, her very being. For years, she could think of little else. The names consumed who she was, took over her psyche. She lost herself for a time; had let the foulness rule her Eve. Let it dictate who she had become. There were many nights she prayed for deliverance.

Then, it happened.

Her power manifested.

It evolved her.

Delivered her from the depths of a mental prison she helped construct for herself.

She had shed her reliance on Eve, became more Lilith.

The power that was at her damn fingertips then was so intoxicating!

Once she decided to write the list, to give visual to the mental, take control over her existence, things began to happen almost immediately. It's funny how fate can play a role in things. Three died of other causes: a fire, a bike accident, and a jealous husband keeping tabs on his cheating wife. Of the remaining four, one was untouchable, Uncle Sam's bitch now, government property, had joined the armed forces and was overseas fighting for his country. He would come later.

That left three. One was incarcerated, would be there for a while. The other two would hold her focus for now. It just happened to work out that they were the two who held the most influence, the most rage that consumed her.

She smiled as she held the instrument that would aid her. It was a simple item really, but sometimes simplicity was what worked the best. Her desires would be fulfilled now.

Soon! Very soon!

She brought it to her face, studied it for a few moments, then placed it over her smile. It transformed her instantly. She could feel its power as she rose. She understood the time had come to bring her plans into the open.

Sugar was born!

$ $ $

Malcolm told his wife of a decade... simply, he would be working late tonight. Working was all he deemed important lately in his busy life . The twins, his wife, his basketball, and golf games, all took a backseat to more pressing matters. Working.

True, he was one of the top sales executives for Wolf and Helms, a company he had helped reach fortune status. His bosses recognized his value and offered him the district manager position for the East Coast with an office based in his hometown of Durham, North Carolina.

His wife wanted him to accept the position without hesitation. It was a chance for them to return home to the Carolinas, a chance she wasn't willing to pass up.

Rochelle never embraced D.C. as Malcolm did. She was a southern girl with southern roots, and that was just the bottom line. From the time he mentioned that promotion, Malcolm had regretted it. Rochelle had applied her not-so-subtle brand of pressure for weeks now. She was the queen of the "withholding tax" method women sometimes employed to get their desired outcome. She wanted out of this city, wanted Malcolm out and free of all the lures and temptations the District had to offer. Rochelle wasn't about to let some younger, freakier, ghetto-booty version of herself bring down and take over all she had worked hard to build.

Malcolm understood these truths about his wife. He just didn't agree with her methods. A man has needs and desires that his chosen mate should fulfill. Period! In Malcolm's mind, Rochelle was failing in some of her womanly and wifely duties. He would miss this life if he submitted to her wants. He would miss the power, the notoriety and most of all, the perks he enjoyed in this city. He had worked hard to cultivate his base of pleasures and respects. He didn't want to start over even if it was in his hometown; where he was already a bit of a local celebrity.

The perks!

His perks were more than mere benefits to him. They included expense accounts, luxury company vehicles, tickets to any event in the area, and a goddess of a personal assistant that Isis herself would feel inadequate compared to. Yes, life was good here, damn good!

Malcolm peered out of his 12th-floor office window and glimpsed the full moon, was awed by its lunar illumination. It gave his and his companion's skin a seductive glow. He marveled at it for a bit. His attention however, was quickly drawn back to his companion and the physical act they were engaged in. Malcolm's breaths were heavy, they grew more ragged with the exertion; muscles tightened and bulged with physical struggle. Sweat beaded his brow as he gave his total focus on the job at hand - a job that had his entire body covered in a heavy sheen of perspiration. Tonight, this white-collar executive had assumed the mantle of a blue-collar worker.

Finishing this most violent of tasks, without getting caught, was the most important "work" he had to complete tonight.

Malcolm wrapped his above-average hands around her throat. It felt so damn good to do so. Then, with the strength of the insane, he began to squeeze. His companion reacted to the physical act with one of her own. She struggled, fought back with her own insanity, refused to give in, to be his victim. She would force her will as well. They existed as two predators, rather than predator and prey.

Malcolm   1

I was in beast mode, a raging savage, savage being the closest word to describe my nature currently on display. The English language did not exist in my speech. Grunts and growls - that was my form of communication. They were the only audible sounds accompanying the echoes of flesh upon flesh.

I was primal. I was predatory. I was reduced to Neanderthal status. I had trapped and corralled my quarry, had her body pinned, head down and round mound up.

Flesh upon flesh, those sounds and scents were damn intoxicating. I eased her all I had to offer and she readily accepted, yielded to me her bountiful treats.

Stacy, my personal assistant, grunted and growled as well, grunted with the movement, with the coupling of flesh, growled with our exercise in sin, with the parting of skins.

In and out…in and out…my cadence was a controlled

rage.

The heat!

The connection!

The damn violence!

I was steady, consistently dropping 10-plus in her wicked womb, which to her credit, she took inch by caramel inch; churning those ample ass hips as she did so.

Mercy…it was not a word that was relevant to me as I was engaged in this violent act, was not given an inch in our embrace of lust. I slammed her, slammed her hard. Our bodies collided with fleshy force, was jackhammering her ass as wave after rippling wave shot through her sweet Georgia peach.

Sounds of applause rang in my ears due to the slapping of our skins. That sound - the primary noise - gave this sexual dance a certain cadence. That rhythm, I used to adjust my gyrations to a more leisurely pace, slowed down the carnage I was inflicting, didn't lessen it, just prolonged the feeling of pleasure pain to her.

Stacy compensated for the shift. Her movements matched my sinful dance. She was the image of an African goddess in all her regal grace, was the embodiment of a Nubian Aphrodite. Her shapely curves gave me some severe visual stimulation as I stroked and choked her into submission. I just continued to ride the waves I was causing. The more I stroked, the more beast-like I became.

The position of the canine, helped to achieve my desired mission of sin.

I had to let the dog out! My arms were more than adequate enough to reach her neck from this position, hands were large enough to close around her throat - bring her to the brink, death and climax, heaven and hell. She loved it that way, made her wetlands even wetter.

Footsteps were falling!

Didn't notice, kept my concentration on the job at hand.

I pulled out, brought my stick of sin to Stacy's face for some oral pleasure.

Needed that…

Loved that…

"No, Malcolm," she said, regaining her voice. "I don't do that. You can sex me any way you want, but I reserve some acts for only my husband; once I snag one."

"Come on, baby," I purred. "Just a little sumtin'…sumtin' to really get me going."

"Not for you or any man unless you put a ring on my finger, then I'll suck you into a coma." Her voice held finality to it.

I sighed, didn't want the same old argument again. I knew I would wear her down eventually. Besides, Stacy had more than enough ass to keep me satisfied until I did. We assumed the position and I went deep again.

Footsteps were falling!

She swept into the room as sudden and as violent as a terrible storm. Hurricane Rochelle had arrived, her thunder being the door to my office slamming against the wall as it was rudely treated. She fixed me and my accomplice in sin-hateful eyes. They spoke murder to us.

Rochelle moved swiftly, her hand trailed lightning as she screamed and flailed her arms about, her lightning being a long, sharp piece of metal that gleamed in the barely visible lunar light. She left traces of shimmering silver in her wake.

Rochelle slowed her advance, menaced us with the butcher's knife she held, became statuesque for a moment. I was still submerged in Stacy, still controlling her movements with my wicked dance, still filling her to capacity. She moved to dislodge me, as she became instantly aware of another presence in the room, an unwanted and unfriendly presence.

I fought to stay, fought her breaking the connection, held her hips and wanted to stay buried in her heat, wanted to finish what was started. I knew I was wrong in so doing but I remained bold. Her heat felt too damn good to release.

"Well, well, Malcolm and his bitch…working," Rochelle screamed, venom dripping with every syllable.

"Baby."

"Shut up! Shut the fuck up, Mal! I knew you were laying that tree-trunk dick of yours somewhere and I figured it was with this ho!"

Stacy cringed at the site and sound of the storm. Rochelle brought the butcher's blade just inches from her attractive and frightened face.

"Please, Mrs. Lee," Stacy whined.

"Please what? Shut the fuck up, ho." Rochelle eyed Stacy, took in her ample curves, her flawless skin, slyly approved. Her eyes roamed a figure that was much like her own, similar complexion, same with height and weight. She nodded. Then Rochelle gave her the smile of the wicked.

I said, "Baby…ungh..." Stacy broke the connection, had me feeling incomplete, had my flesh missing her flesh. She turned, faced me with Rochelle's knife still at her throat.

"Finish him, bitch!"

"Whaaaat...um...finish what, Mrs. Lee?" Stacy asked.

"You know what, ho. I heard you from outside the door. So now you going to do my wifely duties and suck some dick. And, Stacy, I mean suck his shit like your fucking life depends on it." She smiled the smile of the insane. "'Cause it does bitch."

Stacy reluctantly took my still-hardened girth to her lips, then her mouth, next her throat.

"Aaaaah...," I whispered.

"That's it, bitch, get into it, make my bad little boy pleased." Rochelle continued to look on sadistically.

Stacy started slow, slow and steady. Her mouth was surprisingly moist, took her time slobbering inch by caramel inch of me. She made me gasp, reach down grab her head, fuck her face as I had fucked her Eve.

She took her left hand, a southpaw, stroked me while she sucked, did that like a damn professional, like she was a student at Morehead State, getting her Masters. I always figured she was holding out on me, knew she could've always put those motherland lips to work on my wood.

Slow and steady...

Stacy sucked...

Stacy stroked...

Slow and mouth-watering steady...

Stacy's eyes remained opened as she bobbed up and down. Mine were shut. I tried to make this last, wanted to cum but at the same time didn't want to.

Rochelle just watched, looked like she was inspecting,

making sure the job was done right, done to her specifications…done to code.

Stacy looked up, noticed my muscles tighten and tense, knew my climax was coming, knew I was about to blow.

"Milk him, bitch! Milk that big-ass dick that was just fucking the shit out of you!"

Slow and steady…

She whined but remained.

She sucked…

She stroked…

Slow and steady…

I lifted my head and yelled to the heavens while I continued to face fuck my personal assistant with no mercy. Her cheeks bulged, her eyes grew larger. I grabbed a handful of expensive weave, controlled her head as I supervised her mouth.

Stacy's eyes were pleading. They said, no, please don't do this to me. Mine were rolling back in my head.

As my climax took hold, Rochelle grabbed my sac and squeezed. Squeezed and forced volumes upon volumes of liquid bliss from my loins. I shuddered, could barely stand, felt like I was urinating in Stacy's mouth. My pleasure held that much volume. Didn't think I could even produce that amount of jizz.

Ever!

Stacy gagged, let some escape her lovely lips.

"Don't let one drop hit the floor, bitch! Swallow that seed or die!" Rochelle took the hand that wasn't holding the knife and smeared cum that dripped from Stacy's chin on her lips and face. "That's it, Stacy. S-w-a-l-l-o-w!

Stacy obliged, with some difficultly, she coaxed my flow of satisfaction down her throat. I came back to reality then, saw the muscles in Stacy's neck contracting as she swallowed. I glimpsed Rochelle, my wife, my betrothed, my beloved.

Till death do we part!

She gave me a sinful smirk, knew me better than I knew myself. (That pissed me off.) She knew I had just had the orgasm of a lifetime.

Stacy, on the other hand, looked shocked, appalled at being our unwilling participant, our sex slave. She seemed enraged that her consent was not given. I couldn't blame her. Stacy continued to struggle with a mouthful of my love.

"Get to stepping, heifer," my wife said. "Wait!" Rochelle placed the tip of the blade to Stacy's chest.

Paused...

Stared...

Gave eyes of the insane to eyes of the adulterer. She managed to conjure up a mouthful of saliva, spit it all in Stacy's disgusted face. Gravity accomplished the rest, forced it to drip from her chin.

"Now get to stepping, ho, and I hope that taste of dick stays with you for a while because that's the last you'll have of my husband."

As Stacy snatched her clothes and ran out of the office, Rochelle came to me, wicked smile still plastered on her once scowling visage, placed the knife on my desk and kissed me passionately. Her hands roamed my lower front, went to my instrument of sin, began to stroke me slow. She tried to milk what had already been milked. At the moment, it was a lost cause. But I understood.

Till death do we part!

It could never be said that my wife was a quitter. Rochelle refused to give up on my hardness, could tell her desire was rising. She began to succeed in pumping life back into the lifelessness. I felt the tingle again, got so hard and rigid. Her grip tightened, strokes got rapid, kept squeezing with all her insane might.

I was her slave now, here to do her bidding. She had prepped me for her mounting desires.

I understood.

Rochelle let her panties fall to the floor, stepped out of them seductively. She hiked up her hip-hugging skirt, proudly displaying a motherland ass of her own. I gasped, always found my wife's generous curves appetizing and pleasing.

My wife locked eyes with me once more, seemed satisfied with my verbal and physical response to her disrobing. She pushed me back on my desk, mounted my still-Stacy-scented manhood.

Mounted and rode, rode like she was back in the Carolinas on her family's horse farm. I was her wild stallion trying to buck her off, wanting to keep her on.

Rochelle swayed those ample hips, clenched her Kegel muscles to make the fit tight. So damn tight!

I moaned. This was why I was a part of her insanity, why she had a measure of control over me to a point. The fit was so damn tight! Rochelle's Eve quickly became my Garden of Eden.

She was snug and saturated all at once, could dance the dance of the wicked with the simple sway of her hips. She rode me hard, rode me slow, raised that pretty round mound very slow, let it fall oh so fast.

"Oh, shit!" I exclaimed. "Get it, Chelle... get your dick,"

Her gyrations accelerated. Soon we reached a blissful cadence of our own, resided in ecstasy for what seemed like forever. We climaxed in unison, holding each other in a death clench, were eye to eye with primal screams of passion uttered as one.

Till death do we part!

$ $ $

Rochelle began to help me pick up my office. She smoothed her clothes back down, regaining her regal air. She was such a lady that way, had a way of looking picture perfect, almost like royalty. Her beauty was natural, didn't need cosmetics, didn't have to be an illusionist as some women did. She was just naturally fine and physically gifted.

"This has got to stop, Mal. I expect you to call Thompson first thing in the morning and accept the offer."

"Chelle...I...,"

"Malcolm don't...This debate is over, husband of mine, unless you want a fractured family life for your children. I'm taking them home, with or without you." Her tone had finality to it.

"OK, Chelle, point made. I want my family intact." I raised her chin so that we were eye to eye. "You know these little flings mean nothing to me, right? But you have got to stop with punishing me by holding out on that good-ass loving. You know you're my drug and this addict needs his fix."

She smiled wickedly. "Do right and I'll keep that monster between your legs limp and your sac empty." She cupped my testicles as she spoke.

My wife came to me then, embraced me, hugged me full, rested her head on my chest. My arms closed around her. This was the woman I truly loved, the woman I had vowed to forsake all others for. I sighed. It was time to put the toys away and go home.

Time to move to the land of my origin and my first successes, time to reconnect with family and friends, time to make my wife happy again.

It would be good to get the Triplets back together. I couldn't deny the fact that I missed my road dogs. At one point, Deke, Sampson, and I pretty much had the triangle on lock. I knew the Bull City wasn't the District, but it wasn't lacking in beautiful distractions either.

I smiled, thought about the possibilities.

I could make this work, would just have to be a little smarter. One thing I knew, Durham was Rochelle's neck of the woods, as well. She would have eyes and ears every damn where, but that would be part of the fun.

As I stood there holding my wife, my eyes fell on a tiny object lying on the carpet near the door. It grabbed my attention due to its contrast to the color of the carpet.

"Let me go and freshen up, Mal."

I broke our embrace, kissed Rochelle gently, then waited for her to excuse herself to the private restroom in my office. I walked over to the object, picked it up. It was a bright orange piece of plastic. It reminded me of something.

A syringe cap! That was it. I did a quick survey of my office and found the accompanying syringe hiding under my desk. Didn't know how it got there, but I hoped it didn't mean Stacy was shooting up. She had attempted to get me to try Exx with her once, not in pill but liquid form, said it went straight in the blood stream that way, would make the sex that much more explosive. I had declined. This syringe was empty, thank God.

I disposed of both items in my waste basket thinking of Stacy the whole while. Now I was definitely going to miss that Nubian goddess. Stacy was a knockout in every way, probably why I finally succumbed to her advances. She was equal to my wife on every physical level. I'm just glad I finally got to enjoy that sexy-ass mouth of hers before it ended. She was a great personal assistant, and I would make sure she got a glowing letter of recommendation so she would land on her feet elsewhere or with another executive with the company. But bottom line, I had to leave and couldn't take her with me.

Deke 2

I was working, dammit! It was in a shack, a damn hole in the wall. The patrons were damn near elbow to elbow, but, hey, it was work. It was just too bad my cell phone, or more to the point, the fool who kept causing it to vibrate, didn't respect that.

Spinning for the sinning was my trade now. I didn't mind the scene, the atmosphere I found myself in though. Felt at home around all this ghetto booty and overdeveloped ta-tas. All that jiggling made the time pass by more quickly for me. Besides, I was doing more than simply working. A brotha was observing, was learning. I was making mental notes nightly. Watching the enticers, the Oscar-caliber actresses apply their chosen profession. They were the peddlers of fantasy, the dealers of flesh.

As I spun the records, supplying rhythm for the patrons' fleshy muse, I admired their sell game, their dedication to getting that green. Hell, they had to eat, had to feed those ample curves they were peddling. They went on attack mode every night, like sharks in a sea of chum. Lap dancing was done at a premium. I had seen more than a few patrons leave with front-stained pants, left with grins plastered on their faces as wide as the damn Kool-Aid man.

Dancers…umm…strippers or, more to the point, cash-hungry, I'll-bleed-your-wallet-dry females, were not my thing. I didn't knock a nigga for wanting some tits and ass in his face, though, some strange ass and tits. Everybody needs some "strange" sometimes, myself included. I just wasn't into paying for it in a club-type environment.

The damn vibrations in my pants just wouldn't stop! I snatched my cell out of my pocket, eyes falling on the display as I did so. Jackson again! That fat fuck knew I was at work, knew I just got this gig spinning records from the PM to the AM.

Why I had to get an asshole of a PO was beyond me. I guess my luck was still running strong, terrible as ever.

I laid the phone down by my right turntable. Jackson could and would have to wait. He didn't want jack anyway except a damn dime bag of weed. His fat ass couldn't even waste my time for a 20 sac. Funny, I hadn't been out of the county for more than a week, and my so-called probation officer had me dealing again. Now I ain't no damn fool. I let my peeps push the white while I trifled with the green. The green being a hobby of mine was like a little science project for me. I fancied myself a street biologist and was trying to develop a designer strand of weed that would blow one's fucking mind with the minimum of a single damn pull. I wanted to corner the market on that "Loud". I was close to getting it before my little unexpected, all-expense-paid vacation came, compliments of Durham's finest.

Anyway, I wasn't trying to cause any waves so soon. I had just got out of a lot of years on a damn technicality, crucial evidence got missing, thank God. Some would say it was more due to me having friends in the right places. Word on the street was I had become a "snitch bitch."

Wrong!

But it was the only way some of these simple-minded fuckas could explain my lack of jail time. It didn't matter if it were true or not. Rumors in the streets always lead to some type of problem later on.

Truth of the matter was... my boy Sampson had done right by me yet again. He pulled some serious favors, and key evidence mysteriously vanished, along with one main witness. I smiled. It's nothing like having people in your life that you could depend on.

Sampson and me both grew up on the West End of Durham and had kept ties all through public school and college. Yeah, that's right. A nigga went to college, had gone and played ball, as a matter of fact. I had a full ride until I got caught up in a little off-the-court trouble...girl problems. I was the victim of some false rape allegations that got cleared up later. But by the time the smoke cleared, the damage had been done to my playing career.

I still reminisce about those glory days with me, Malcolm, and Sample. The Triplets is what they used to call us. We led Central to its first college basketball championship. Shit, there was kitty on a platter for all of us on that team. White, black, and fine-ass Mamacitas. We had the Triangle on lock!

The display on my phone lit up again. I couldn't hear it due to the head phones I was wearing. Jackson again! I was trying to get my playlist together for tomorrow, did it the old school way with the vinyl. Don't get me wrong, I had state-of-the art equipment, laptop and mp3s that I could easily interface with the club's sound system, but it was something about actually spinning that made this feel like a real job to me, so I indulged myself.

Me a working man –well, it's a start at least. I hadn't held a steady gig since I worked at the Internet Sweepstakes spot on University Drive, was security there. This job was different. I made sure I carefully observed this business from the inside out. The owner, Black, was a distant cousin of mine, and while in lockup, we talked about job opportunities for me. He told me about this shack, which I had frequented before. Told me about his number-one money maker, too: Sugar. He made it clear that in his unchallenged opinion, she was the sexiest creature on the planet. Said her sweat could be bottled up and niggas would buy it. Also told me she was a strange one. He said Sugar was mysterious, said she was a little insane. She wore a snow-white wig with black streaks, wore white contacts that gave her the look of a sexual vampire and most importantly, she wore these expensive-looking Mardi Gras/masquerade-type masks. Sugar was never seen at the club without those props. Black smiled to himself. He said he admired her game even though she kept her identity hidden. The masks she wore usually covered half her face, but you could tell there was some serious beauty underneath them. But even so, with that traffic-stopping body of hers, there wasn't too many folks paying that much attention to her face, if you get my meaning.

I had studied Black's face as he revealed this information about Sugar to me. Had never seen him, for lack of a better word, respect someone the way he did this stripper. I asked Black had he ever seen Sugar without the mask. He just gave me a look that told me to drop it, told me what he deemed important for me to know. He stressed to me that I should keep an eye on his most prized recruit. I agreed. There were worse jobs to have than working in a strip club and keeping tabs on its headliner.

I secretly had my own plans anyway. This was the perfect apprenticeship for me. I just had to lay low and observe.

Sugar finished her set about an hour ago. As the headliner, she was the last to go on and required more music than the others. I'll be damned if there wasn't a soft dick in the hiss-ouse— after all of that ghetto-ass got done jiggling, including mine!

Sugar…huh. The name suited her just fine. She just looked sweet to the taste. Damn! Sugar wore sugar: sugar-made pasties, with sugar cubes covering her perky nipples. She had a thin chain of sugar cubes around her waist, which she let a few patrons nibble and bite from as she gyrated in their faces. Sugar didn't wear glitter on her creamy mocha skin but instead chose to wear actual sugar crystals that she attached with honey. Original as a muthafucka! She definitely went all in on this name.

If I had to describe what she was working with and why

she was such a draw, I would say that simply, she just had a way of bringing out pure sexual arousal from anyone who gazed at her for any length of time. Whether you were a dog or a cat, got hard or wet, Sugar had that effect on your carnal desires. She had motherland curves, generous and ample in all the right places. Had a creamy-butter complexion and a hypnotizing gaze that I'm sure was enhanced from the contacts, but that didn't detract from her overall sex appeal. I took her to be a supreme actress who knew her audience very well and played to their wants.

I periodically found myself wondering who she really was if you lifted her illusion. She was familiar to me for some odd reason. I made a promise to myself to find out more about her, find out what made her tick. I just had to play it right.

Shit, I couldn't wait for her to stroll out of the dressing room and sway her sexy ass my way to discuss her song selections for the next night.

I always waited for Sugar to dress. She was always the last dancer to leave. I would

routinely dismiss security, with their non-professional asses. They eagerly left her to my protection. (Black had obviously sanctioned it.) Sugar's body was my responsibility, and I took her safety very seriously. She appreciated that about me and as a result, I was one of the few people, outside of her customers, who she gave any of her attention to. Sugar startled me as I was packing up and putting my music away. She appeared at the DJ booth a few feet from the stage.

"Hey, Deke," she purred.

Just the speaking my name from her full lips was enough to have me growing instantly.

"What up, Sugar," I said coolly.

"Is your last name Wonder or something?"

"Huh?"

"I've given you sign after sun-blazing, fucking sign, and you act like you ain't seen shit."

I grinned. "Well damn, Sugar, just thought you were being friendly."

"Nigga, please! Have you ever seen me be friendly to anyone up in this liquor house that wasn't giving up their family's bill money just to have a chance to sniff this pussy."

Sugar was raw, but was still not vulgar to me, in her delivery. It had to do with the sultry voice she possessed, I guessed. She had that natural breathy tone of a phone sex operator without the fakeness. It was just smooth in a sing-song type of way.

I nodded my head, had to agree with her. Sugar didn't waste her time with idle chatter which was why the other dancers hated her guts, though they all envied her game.

She winked. "Well tell me, Stevie...can you see me now?"

"Can't miss you," I replied.

"I felt a little edgy tonight, turned myself on I guess, and I'm not really ready to go home just yet. Are the two bumbling brutes masquerading around as security still here?"

"Nope. They took off about 20 minutes ago, and Jeff, the so-called club manager, took off a little bit before they did. It's just you and me here now."

"Really… just you and little ole me, alone?" Sugar slinked over to the bar. "Have a drink with me, Deke?" she asked.

"Sugar, you know I don't drink"

She smiled. "Yeah, I kinda like that about you. You seem to keep a clear and level head all the time. It's like you don't want to be surprised by anything." She poured herself a drink, looked to be a double. "You don't like surprises much, do you, Deke?"

"Depends on the surprise," I answered.

She smiled. "Have you ever been Hen-sucked, Deke?"

"Hen…what?"

"Sucked, Deke. Hen sucked."

Sugar eyed me, stared at the bottle of liquor she held. She poured herself another drink, that act being seductive and sexual alone. I continued to pack my music not wanting to stare.

"Well, are you going to answer me or not?"

"Can't say that I have, Sugar. I'm almost afraid to ask…but… are you offering?"

"Maybe," she smiled. She explored my body then, eyes roamed up then down, stopped and focused on my southern region.

"Yeah, I believe we could have a little fun tonight if you can handle it and keep your mouth shut."

"Bring it on then, Sugar." I tried to contain my internal big-ass grin. Was finally going to see if Sugar was all show or could she do what her body suggested in her performances.

She poured and downed half of another drink, started advancing my way, raised her glass. "Yeah, my two favorite browns: dick and Hennessy!" She grinned, displaying a perfect set of ultra-white teeth. "I noticed you noticing me for weeks now, Deke. Why haven't you made a move on me like the rest of these fools up in here?"

"Good things cum to those who wait," I answered. Hoped Sugar picked up on the double meaning.

"Play some slow Janet for me," Sugar demanded.

I quickly found a collection of slow jams by Ms. Jackson and hurriedly had her melodies wafting from the club's speakers.

Sugar swayed to the melody, made a gesture as if she was about to remove her mask, acted like she would privilege me to see her perfection. Sugar was just teasing, though. She smiled as she moved, a smile that took in her entire face, looked so feline. She migrated with the grace of a cat, the sure footedness of pussy, had mastered her God-given gifts, knew how to gyrate portions of her body that would illicit the desired response from the opposite sex.

I swallowed hard, felt heat rise to my face, felt other parts of my anatomy rise as well. Sugar stood just 10 feet from me but by the time she covered half that distance, my dick could've cut diamonds. I was that fucking hard!

Janet continued to croon while Sugar continued to advance. Though she was still fully dressed, I found her to be even more appealing to my senses. I had practically seen all of her naked glory while she worked, but this was different. Covered, Sugar still held a certain mysteriousness, a curiosity to me.

She then eased into my space, spoke to me with that breathy sultry voice. I invited the closeness, inhaled her once minty breath that held the scent of expensive alcohol now, savored her spicy fragrant perfume.

It was all strangely familiar.

"Relax, Deke," she cooed. "Let Sugar sweeten you up a bit."

I took my shirt off, leaned back in my swivel chair, let her hand roam my chest, my mid-section, then she lingered on my Adam.

She took another shot of Henny, poured some in my belly button. I was an innie. She swirled her tongue around my flesh-made cup, slurped up the remaining, had me feeling even more aroused, didn't even think that was possible.

Sugar looked at me longingly, always with the eye contact, this one was. She allowed the residual alcohol to stream further down my mid-section, let it pool around my Adam. Sugar traced, followed the flow with her probing tongue, lapped up the excess and took me to some serious humidity. Her mouth was smoldering, on fire, *en fuego*. She let me camp there for a few seconds enjoying the heat.

"Aaaaaah," I moaned. All I could do was sit there, didn't know what heaven on earth was, but I knew what I was experiencing had to be close. Sugar snaked her tongue around my Adam, made me squeal like Eve. She covered my 'shroom with a hood of hotness, that being her saturated mouth. Didn't bob, just made her head dance north and south, let it sway east and west.

No hands!

Sugar was a fucking pro, had me speaking in tongues while her tongue spoke to me.

She stopped abruptly, looked at me. "You like?" she asked.

"Yes," was all I managed to murmur, trying with all my might to keep from busting right then and there.

She must've read my expression because she relinquished my member, pulled back a bit. Sugar smirked, took another shot, put the hood back over me.

Started slow…

Kept it gradual...

Never been stroked like that before. Sugar sucked me with her unusually long and talented tongue, felt like wet hands were wrapped around my dick.

Kept it slow…

Janet was singing "Anytime" in my ear while Sugar had my other senses on lock and as I listened, I was thinking, now dammit! The time is now!

I erupted, didn't cum, couldn't call it that. I literally dropped a sexual nuke, could picture my mushroom cloud inside Sugar's mouth.

"Gaaaaad!" I howled.

Sugar never stopped.

Kept it slow…

Milked me dry to the point of making me faint. That was the last memory I had.

Before…

I vaguely remember a loud buzzing sound as I drifted in and out of reality.

Never came like that.

Ever…

When I returned to the living, I was lying on the floor of the club. My pants were down around my ankles. Sugar was gone. Didn't remember her leaving, didn't understand why or how I had been left alone but one thing I did know, Sugar had left me weak, had left me alone, but she had left me very satisfied!

$ $ $

Boom…boom… boom! The base was hitting so hard I could barely concentrate on the record I was spinning. A week had passed since my little escapade with Sugar. She only worked twice a week at this club, so I hadn't received an opportunity to corner her and ask about the disappearing act. To tell the truth, I was a bit embarrassed. I had never passed out due to an orgasm, weed and liquor yes (which was why I'd quit such indulgences) but never from nutting too hard. I was still a little unnerved by the whole thing.

Boom! Boom! Sugar was on deck, hips undulating to the baseline. She made each ass cheek dance independently to the music. Made her tongue writhe like a serpent, had the audience hypnotized, the working included.

Sugar had the men hard, the women wet, and her coworkers dripping with envy. I couldn't shake that reappearing thought that something about her was strangely familiar, felt that way the first time my eyes lingered on her edible frame. It was more her mannerisms than anything else. I just couldn't put my finger on it, though.

Oh well. It really didn't matter. I had more important shit to focus on, like getting my boys to invest in a new club.

It would be a goldmine if done right. All I need is a sure-fire headliner and as my eyes casually fell toward the stage, with Sugar being...well...Sugar, I had a clear vision of the glory I could attain if I partnered up with this most incredible sexual creature.

Stealing Sugar from Black could and would be a bit tricky as well as extremely risky. I knew she was loyal to him because she could've left this dive a long time ago but she kept working her two nights a week. I didn't know their connection, especially with Black in lockup, but it had to be pretty tight. I just knew I had to persuade her, knew after the other night, she found something about me pleasing, just had to capitalize on that somehow and keep my freaking head after.

One didn't just cross Black!

Ever!

I kept telling myself to look at the gains, grab a slice of life, to carve out a legitimate future for myself. I wanted to be a real businessman. I was tired of being the street version. This club idea of mine could be my ticket out of the hustling game. Period!

As I mulled over all the possibilities, Sugar finished her set and sashayed her sweet ass through the crowd. Every head up in there was eye fucking the hell out of her as she did so. I observed this performance as well. All I saw was dollar signs. Cha-ching like a muthafucka! Sugar was a natural at working the crowd. The way she maintained eye contact, her not-so-subtle placement of her hands and feet, the voice that purred into the ears of her monetary victims as she gently massaged their southern regions containing their egos. She could literally coax hundreds from broke niggas' pockets. Cha-ching!

All I had to do was entice, enthrall, and pretty much ensnare Sugar in my little web.

Sugar made eye contact with me as she waded through the sea of men and women trying to pay for her current attention. Her eye contact was strong, got me to thinking. She smiled my way, could tell we would talk later by her gaze. Sugar wanted something. I just had to give her what she wanted so I could get what I wanted. It was still difficult for me to get the image of her blessing me with that sexually skilled mouth of hers. She seemed to enjoy kneeling at my altar almost as much as I did.

Damn!

That was the best skull a nigga had in years. She-it, who am I fooling…ever!

"What up, Deke," Sugar purred.

"Nothin', Shugs. You were on fire tonight, sexy. But that's hardly anything new, now is it? I could barely keep my eyes off your…assets tonight."

She grinned. "You recover from your coma yet. Sorry I had to leave you in that state, but I had an emergency to attend to."

"Naw …Shug. That was on me. Never passed out form a BJ before. Damn, girl, what did you do to me?"

"Yeah, Deacon, I know I got skillzzz," she teased. Sugar eyeballed me up and down, leaving little mystery as to her intentions.

"How 'bout we finish what we started the other night. I didn't get the chance to lay these walls, these sugar walls on that Carolina black snake of yours."

"Yeah, I got some shit to lay on you as well," I stated.

Sugar nodded. "OK, Deke, round two is on. Hope you trying to go for a knockout this time around."

I smiled, showing off my pearly whites. That gets them all the time, leaned in closer to her then, inhaled her sweet fruity scent, brushed past her face to her ear, blew ever so slightly before I spoke. "Ride home with me tonight. We can get your car in the morning."

"Why don't I just follow you home, Deke?"

"Naw, trying to be a gentleman here," I lied. I didn't want or need her whip being seen at my place.

"Gentleman...I don't need no gentle-ass-man tonight. What I need is a 'I been on lockdown for 90-plus days' dick!"

I knew my grin was as wide as my face, but I couldn't help it.

"Can you handle that, Deke? Yes or no?"

"Get your shit," I damn near yelled. "Cause we are out!"

Sampson   3

"Watts he's crossing over Holloway and heading into the Keys," I yelled into my walkie-talkie. Watts was my partner, was fairly new on this patrol, Watts had gotten a shock when I spotted a perp who didn't want to see me. I gave chase on foot, when the fool bolted.

Damn! I couldn't believe this muthafucka was going to make me chase his stupid ass. My adrenaline was already pumping, coursing through my veins the moment I caught sight of Bones' delinquent ass. I'm going to make his ass pay double what he owes, maybe even triple what I usually charge to keep such dealers out of the county.

"Copy that, Sampson," Watts said, breaking my contemplations.

Bones was usually a reliant two yards a week, but he had slacked off here lately. He was small time but, hey, he still had to pay to play. Yeah, I knew the drug division of the Durham P.D. was cracking down on crack. (Now that's funny.) But that ain't my damn problem; it's theirs.

You want to slang on my side of town, you pay the fee or I bust your sorry no-job-having ass.

Bones…they should call his anorexic-looking ass Gonzalez, for Speedy. He ran across Holloway Street into Turnkey, what some Durhamites call the Keys. Fool thought he would lose me in the neighborhood. Please! I grew up hanging over here with my cousins: Shon and Big Mike.

I cut through two yards, cut his dumbass off, and tackled his surprised ass like I was back in a Northern Knights uniform wreaking havoc on high school quarterbacks. As I think back on things, I should've stayed with the football thing, but no, I had to follow Malcolm and Deke to school and play the round ball. At 6'4 250 pounds of mean-ass cop, I could still bring the pain when need be.

Bones folded damn near in half as I speared through his body. The collision was vicious. I had more than knocked the wind out of him, probably cracked a few ribs as well. He struggled to breathe. Pain crept across his terrified face as he exhaled. I yanked his ass up by the back of his neck causing him to shriek in pain, shook him violently then, to make my point at him to be quiet, next I turned him so he faced me. He whimpered. "So…you late again, Derrick," I raged. "Why-tha-fuck did you make me break a sweat chasing your dumbass, huh?"

"Come on—Sample," he said.

"Officer Sampson to you, nigga. My friends, my family, and my bitches call me Sample. You are neither."

He nodded his understanding then coughed, was really

struggling to breathe now. "My bad," he croaked.

"You got-damn right, it's your bad, Derrick!"

"I…I'll have your money on Friday, Samp—I mean, Officer Sampson. I swear!" Bones trembled like he was freezing. He wasn't shaking due to the cold, was rather because he knew.

I said, "Friday…nigga, it's Tuesday, and Friday will be two weeks late." I eyed his fear rising as I spoke. I frowned, could smell it on him like a canine would. "Besides, Derrick, it's too late for that now."

He struggled and said, "No, Sample, I swear on my kids…please, man, I'll have it Friday."

"Heard you been talking Bones. Heard that mouth of yours suffering from a case of diarrhea and I ain't talking 'bout yo' stank-ass breath either."

"Talking?" He feigned ignorance. "Talking to who, Samp? Naw, man…not me."

"To them damn I.A. fuckers. You know who the hell I'm talking about. I heard you got picked up a week ago and dropped my name quick as a two-dollar ho drops her dirty ass drawz."

I gave the fool a chance to tell me the truth, not sure why, didn't really matter to me one way or the other, but I gave him the chance anyway. I saw lies all over his face, saw his pathetic brain working, trying to get him out of the inevitable.

He pleaded. "Sample, I ain't said shit to no AI or any other alphabets. I wouldn't—,"

He never finished, due to my having him in a choke hold in mid-sentence. His eyes bulged, breathing became even more ragged. Didn't really have the time to end him this way. Choking someone to death isn't as quick and easy as they make it seem in the movies. It takes a hell of a lot longer, and time was definitely not on my side at the moment.

Watts, my partner, would be pulling up soon. She was too damn cute to foot it out like I had, so she went for the squad car as my predictable chase scenario played out. Figured I had a couple of minutes tops before she found us or radioed for backup. With that knowledge running through my head, I made my decision or rather it was made for me.

I gave Bones a smashing head butt crumpling him to the ground then picked up his 140 pounds of dead weight, got him in a choke hold from behind and cut off his air supply permanently. Fortunately for me, we were just a few yards away from the park that was connected, but not actually in the Keys. It was really just a small basketball court with one bench placed in a hollow in the woods. The park had almost been covered by those woods and brush. (Durham Parks & Recs at its finest) Shit…this couldn't get any easier.

I put the now limp body of Bones over my shoulder, carried him to the bench that was the only place to sit at the courts, propped him up like he was just lounging, chilling for the last time he was.

I decided to search him one last time, found a crumpled and wet hundred in his left sock.

"You lying fuck," I spat. I guess you can't trust anybody these days to tell you the fucking truth. I kicked the corpse in the side. "Thanks for the contribution."

Took off running at top speed up Lynn Road, crossed over Holloway again, and made it to an old housing community before I radioed Watts to come pick me up.

When Watts pulled up, I was leaning against a tree in someone's front yard.

"Need a lift, stranger," she asked. Watts shined our patrol car's spotlight on me, made the light slowly scan my body from head to toe.

"Kill the light, Watts," I said. I eyed her face. She was smiling, and that act alone got me aroused. I was already pumped, and it didn't take much. Not for the first time I was glad Jones, my former partner, got a permanent vacation and Watts became my new partner.

Watts…she wasn't the prettiest, didn't have the phattest ass or the biggest set of knockers, but she had a generous amount of all the goodies a man would want and was well toned with it - workout fucking queen. What did stand out about her aside from her strawberry blonde hair and Carolina-blue eyes, was her bomb- (and I do mean bomb) ass fellatio. Watts should give oral lessons! Shit!

We cruised over to one of our spots for some on duty booty. Old Farm Park was near pitch black at night, very few lights at the entrance and practically none (that were working) once you get in the heart of the area. We pulled all the way down to the basketball courts, jumped in the backseat. I handcuffed her and undressed her roughly, just like she liked it. It took maybe one minute before I had her toned and tanned white ass in the buck, legs on my shoulders, her feet were arched, toes pointed at awkward angles.

"Get…it…Sample…g-get… it!" Her voice was choppy. She fought back with her hips as I pounded her hard and deep. I was committing battery all up in her vanilla snatch.

Watts and I had been fucking since the sergeant paired us four months prior. The attraction and chemistry was almost instant. I had been fucked and sucked on almost every secluded road or out-of-the way spot on our patrol; damn near all of Durham.

She-it…life was good. All I had to do was knock her back out, and her clueless ass stayed in the dark about my side dealings while we were on duty. Once, I actually thought she had figured me out, was gonna turn snitch, rat my ass out to internal affairs. But as luck would have it, she just used the information she had gathered to blackmail me into giving her a steady supply of this snake. For real! She actually thought she had to use leverage on me to tear that ass up on the regular. Now I must admit, she was a bit crazy, but everyone knows crazy cat is the best cat.

Watts was two kinds of crazy. She was protective over this dick and extremely jealous. I knew this thing: us fucking, would eventually end badly. Shit, this bitch was about the only chick I knew I had to ration the dick to.

I had to keep her on a short leash, had to keep her from tasting my almond joy too much, didn't need or want her going psycho while we were on duty. Watts craved my shit, couldn't get enough of this chocolate. To be honest, that damn vanilla was pretty addictive as well.

"Give me a Sample and the whole goddamn plate," Watts moaned.

I was on my next-to-the-last down stroke when my phone started vibrating, got a text from Deke saying he wanted to meet up in the morning. It had to be something serious cause that nigga usually didn't wake or rollover till noon at the earliest.

"Aaaaaah...God Watts," I screamed.

"Give it up, you big black muthafucka!"

I busted all up in her ass for the umpteenth time. Watts was fixed, had been spade or neutered, whichever. She didn't want or need any kids. Ever! That was what she made clear to me the first time I went there with her. That just made our fornicating all the more enjoyable, flesh to flesh, skin to skin, I was constantly dumping buckets of nut in that tight juicy ass twizz –aat, like I was doing right at the moment.

Hey, duty calls!

Malcolm　　　4

I was exhausted. It had been three weeks since my family and I had relocated back to the Carolinas, Durham to be exact.

We had found a house at an affordable (in my wife's mind) price, and Rochelle and her kitty-following friends had been having a ball spending my money furnishing the place.

I had actually walked in on a conversation of theirs a couple of days ago that confirmed my assessment of Rochelle returning to her Queen "B" status. Rochelle and a group of her friends, including her somewhat best friend, Claudia, were having a heated discussion over cheating men; specifically Claudia's. I almost walked in on them when I entered the house from the garage area. Almost. I stayed back and easedropped a little.

"Yeah girl, the point is, if you want your dog to stay at home at least most of the time, you got to feed him lean meat instead of fat and grissle." They all laughed at the speaker. It sounded like my wife's voice.

"Excuse me…"

"You heard me bitch…put down that freaking mac-n-cheese and go get your fat ass a gym membership Claudia. Or not. Just be prepared for your man to keep chasing skirts who look more like me. That's just my two damn cents."

"I don't recall asking for your fucking two cents. Bitch you aint all that. What… now you going to tell us that prettyboy Malcolm aint stepping out on your skinny ass."

I leaned in closer to listen better. "Oh, no bitch, I'm not saying that at all." I could picture Rochelle fixing Claudia with a smug expression. "What I'm saying tubby is he takes care of his wife and home very well. That he pays to play so to speak. I wouldn't be with no broke-ass-muthafucka like Dallas and let that shit slide, that's for fucking sure."

I peeked around the corner, Claudia looked to be on the verge of battling. She was a robust woman and I had concerns if Rochelle could take her if it came to that. Rochelle's other girlfriends were silent doing this exchange, probably didn't want Rochelle's wrath aimed their way.

"Fuck you Ro! Money aint everything…"

"Yeah Claudia, it's the only thing and if you think otherwise, go ahead and marry that deadbeat and see how happy you'll be when he's fucking a better looking bitch while your dumb ass is footing all the bills."

Claudia got up and stormed out of the front door. I just barely got out of sight when she did so. Rochelle rushed to the front door and yelled, " Bitch please, you better wake the fuck up! And Claudia…"

Claudia turned to face Ro as she was getting in her car."What?" She said vexed.

"Lose some damn weight!"

Claudia burned rubber in our driveway, couldn't leave fast enough. Hey, that's Rochelle.

I was glad when they left to go shopping. Whatever it took to keep her attention distracted from my comings and goings was just fine with me. She stayed and enjoyed being busy with such things. I needed some me time as well.

It was a Tuesday in mid June, which meant near-90-degree weather in the Triangle. The sun had been beaming all day, but as it set, the heat became tolerable at least.

I had worked a few hours over to avoid getting cooked and, truthfully, because that is what I do. I have always worked hard and played harder. Later, I planned to unwind with the fellows. I had told Deke we could hang for a bit and then I would take him to work.

I pressed the button on my wireless key to start up the Jaguar I bought when I returned to the area. I was looking forward to driving again. I really didn't drive much while I lived in the District. I went ahead and dropped the top down on the convertible, took off my tie, and loosened my collar. Free at last!

I dialed Deke's cell phone. "Yo, negro, I'm on the way," I said. "Please be ready, 'cause you know you always have either me or Sample waiting on your slow ass."

"Hey, what's the rush? Anyway, I'm already ready,

need to make a quick stop if you don't mind then I'll be ready to wipe your ass from the ceiling to the floor in a friendly game of billiards."

I grinned. "You always talking shit. We'll see, little man."

"OK, see you soon, bro."

Deke was still Deke, but I noticed he was a little different lately, more driven. I like to see that in my brother from another mother, wanted to see him prosper. He had been through a lot after his father died while he was in college. Deke had been raised in a single-parent home with his father. Mr. Jones was a father figure and big brother to both me and Sampson. We all took a huge hit to the heart the day he died, and, of course, Deke took it the worse. He had fallen in with his drug-dealing ass cousins, and it was all downhill from there.

Sample was meeting us later at Deke's job. Job! Deke with a job now, what was the world coming to? But I was proud... proud because he was. Funny how employment can make a man feel like a man. There is nothing like being a contributing member of society. Anyway, as I pulled into the BP on Roxboro, my attention was drawn to a couple of sistas dressed for the heat, tops covering little, shorts covering even less.

God bless the Carolinas!

One was wearing a red top with the word J-U-I-C-E-Y wrapped around her boobs in white letters, the other, a white top with the same moniker in red. Red top, the driver, eyeballed me and my ride as I eased my Jag in the spot adjacent to hers, didn't say anything, just stared. I stared back, let her read my thoughts through my gaze, took in her generous breasts that were frantically trying to escape that way-too-tight top. Cleavage galore!

I let my eyes drift downward. Her ass definitely put the apple in apple bottom, had a flat, toned stomach with outrageous T and A. Her stance did everything it could to accentuate her God- and mother-given assets. Basically this chick was a walking sexual advertisement. I looked her up and down and started growing, didn't have the heart to tell her that there was no "E" in Juicy, but I digress.

"Nice ride," I said, breaking the ice.

"You too," she responded. "What's your name, pretty boy?"

I answered, "Malcolm...yours?"

"Benzi," she said.

I made a feeble attempt to act like I was looking over her vehicle, an older model Mercedes with new rims. Really...Benzi, I get it, you got a Benz. After suppressing a gut- busting bout of laughter, I decided to play this out to see if I could get confirmation as to the type of women I was dealing with. Strippers would be my guess.

"Bet that car rides nice as well," I grinned.

She smiled. "Not as well as I do."

"Benzi, you know we running late," her friend in the white top exclaimed, irritated I hadn't acknowledged her yet.

I faced white top then. "Oh—and how are you doing today, bonita," I said, giving the Latina sidekick intense roving eyes.

"Fine," she blushed.

"What are you lovely ladies about to get into--"

"Work," White top said.

"Work?" I eyed them again. Bingo! I could well guess the type of job they had, dressed as they were.

"Yeah, work, negro," she smiled "You should come to see us there sometime."

"Oh, where's work," I asked.

White top reached in the glove box, pulled out a black business card, pressed some sexy full lips to the back, leaving her red lipstick mark on. She then exited the passenger side, sauntered the whole two feet separating us, leaned in resting her well-developed breasts in my driver-side window and handed me the card. She smiled just inches from my face, could smell her perfume, was surprisingly light and sweet, a pleasant aroma contrasting the loud apple scent of the bubblegum she continued to chew in my face.

"Blacks," I read out loud.

"Yeah, pretty boy. Come check us out. We more than worth it." That was still white top speaking.

"It's a date," I said still eyeballing Benzi with white top in my face.

"It can be whatever you want it to be, lover. I'm Tracie. You met Benzi," she said, gesturing toward red top.

"Tracie and Benzi, OK. What do you ladies do at Blacks?"

They each smirked at one another. "Why dance the dance, silly boy," they both said in somewhat-practiced unison.

I looked at the card again. Strippers with business

cards, I thought. You gotta love it.

"Hope you come on through tonight, Malcolm," Benzi said with measured breathy tones. She eyed me seductively. "Save a lap dance for you, pretty boy, if you do."

"Fine by me," I answered licking my lips.

They pulled off, and I went inside the station to get something cool to drink.

When I exited the store, I saw a complete blacked-out SUV (maybe a Tahoe) parked a little ways from the pump. Thought I saw the same truck in the parking lot at work, then on the highway when I was on my way to get gas.

Strange.

I knew damn well Rochelle wasn't having me followed already. It couldn't be. Yes, it could. It was probably just my imagination working overtime though. Damn, there were plenty of black-on-black trucks rolling around in Durham. I must have been tripping. I pumped my gas then left to go get Deke.

The black truck pulled off just a few seconds before I did

Sampson 5

I was exiting my home when I saw the scum.

A damn all-black, dark-tinted windows, four-door, SUV parked a few houses down the street from mine. Damn internal affairs fucks! Off or on duty, they were intent on shadowing and fucking with my ass.

I looked up, nodded in their direction, gave them a one-finger salute before entering my vehicle. Held it aloft, so that they could clearly see I had noticed them. I didn't get any type of response to my obscene gesture. I knew they saw, though.

I was on my way to meet Deke and Mal. Shit, I can't lie. That black truck had me nervous. Got to thinking, maybe I needed a little something to take my mind off of this shit.

I almost picked up my cell to call Watts. Almost! Wanted to maybe get a quickie in real quick, but, hey, what was I thinking? Hell, I was going to a damn strip club! If I can't get my mind off things there with all that scattered ghetto ass around, nothing would do the trick.

I called Watts anyway to set up some after-club action. I got her voicemail. "Watts—it's Sample." Fuck! I hate leaving messages. "Get back with me when you can, got something important to discuss with you."

As I disconnected the call, I glanced in my rearview mirror, saw that damn truck once more. It stayed with me for a few exits then vanished. Fuck!

Hell, when I get to Black's little hole in the wall, I'm going to order two doubles from the jump.

I found it a little unnerving that Watts hadn't answered when I called. That was not her norm, couldn't remember the last time she failed to answer on the first damn ring. She always seemed overly eager and ready to get at this snake.

I smiled. Me and Watts were starting to make a pretty good team. I already knew I could trust the crazy bitch. She could've had my ass in a sling on several occasions if she wanted. Watts never did. I was thinking of letting her in, showing her my side jobs, wanted to make her a partner in more ways than one. Yeah, me and Watts running shit. I could get used to a little milk in my coffee. I called again, went straight to voicemail this time. Damn!

I pulled into the parking lot of Black's, noticed Mal's Jaguar right away, rich muthafucka. It looked a bit out of place among the other vehicles in the lot. Patrons had their ghetto mobiles proudly on display. Most were older luxury cars (bought around tax time, no doubt) with brand new shiny rims. Mal's Jag was a reflection of him, elegant and polished with some serious power under the hood. Malcolm was a refined brotha who had managed to escape the streets but still held his cred'. Make no mistake, he was still hood to his core, just put a nice suit on top of it. He had had my back on too many occasions to count, trust me. He was no punk, far from it. I knew his truth despite his professional outward persona. The Triplets were brothers through and through, and you couldn't fuck with one without fucking with the other two. We had some wild times, let me tell you...

Black's club was a damn smokehouse! Visibility was a problem until you got used to the weed, cigar, and cigarettes sharing the air with your eyes and lungs. It streamed out the front door as I was let in, had to let my eyes adjust to the dark and the smog. I stifled a cough and noticed the tits and ass on full display as I entered.

The bartender and wait staff were topless. Black's sported an all-girl staff except for security and the DJ. Damn! I nodded to some of the security, recognized a few of the brutes. They were off-duty officers. They appeared to have found a pie-ass side job. Working around all the tits and ass you could stand isn't a bad way to earn some extra dough.

Black was a jailbird genius, and obviously knew how to appeal to a brotha's wallet. I'm sure money flows more freely with big ass tits in your face along with some potent alcoholic drinks.

I caught sight of Mal sitting at a table with a bottle of something expensive, I'd wager. He was flanked on both sides by two fine-ass flesh peddlers. One had her hand in his pants, stroking. The other had her boobs in his face trying successfully to breast feed his grown ass. He looked like he was enjoying himself, if not amusing himself.

"Mal, what up, brotha man," I said.

"Samp, come sit down, man. I want you to meet some new friends of mine, Benzi and Tracie." He gestured to the one still gripping his dick. "Tracie, this is Sampson, one of my brothers." He stuck a couple of benji's in her thong. "Hook him up with one of your vicious lap dances. I'm buying."

Tracie flashed me a devilish smile, crossed the empty space between us gyrating her voluptuous hips as she did so. She allowed her ass to submit to the rhythm of the music that I had failed to notice up until now. I took in her curves. Nice. She had red tassels hanging from redbone breasts. A red, white and blue thong saluted not the good ole US of A, but rather she was reppin' its possession, Puerto Rico.

"Tracie…huh," I asked, my eyes falling and remaining on her thong.

"Stage name, was given to me by Black. He said I reminded him of her; somebody he used to bang, I guess. You can call me Carmen, Papi."

I approved.

Latino heat!

"Come to Papi, mamacita," I said.

"Aye Papi. Carmen please you."

I gave Mal a thumbs up while Carmen sat on my lap facing Mal and his kitty. She gripped me with her cheeks through my slacks. I took a drink, let my head fall back and relished the sweet sensation of new flesh on my lap.

"Let's go to the back," Carmen purred in my ear.

Deke gave us a shout out over the microphone as Carmen led me to a back room that she referred to as the "Blackout." Their version of the champagne room, I guess. The room was, of course, pitch black, I could barely make out the faux leather sofas propped against the back wall. Carmen pushed me down on one. I noticed the walls were actually glass, dark-tinted glass but glass nonetheless. My guess was security was watching whatever went on in the room, but they didn't stop whatever the dancers wanted to do like they did in the upscale clubs.

"What does Papi want?" Carmen asked as she pulled my slacks down around my ankles, had her hands in my boxer briefs. She freed what was confined there and I could see her surprise even in the near darkness; heard her gasp.

"Grande," she whispered. "Let me taste all the meat." Carmen shifted from Spanish to English without hesitation, as if she mixed the two languages together.

"Taste all you like, but I'd rather you make a meal of this veal." I grabbed the base of my dick, squeezed, made the head swell to massive proportions, wanted to see what her reaction would be to my move.

Carmen smiled, then went to work! I knew better than to interrupt an artist while they worked so I decided to lie back and enjoy. I ignored the vibrating in my pants pocket, was vibrating since I entered the room. Carmen was all I had brain power to focus on now anyway. If it was an emergency, they would leave a voicemail or call back.

Carmen stopped, climbed on, put her tongue in my

mouth. She tasted minty. "I don't do this usually," she breathed into my ear. "But I got to feel all this up in me." She eased what I figured had to be a Magnum on my meat, (that fit was even tight) then lowered herself slowly as if she were testing the temperature of hot bath water. Once Carmen got one fourth of me in, she moaned." Never had this much man in me....oh...n-e-v-e-r." She took me slow at the beginning, then got her confidence, fucked me hard and fast, screaming in English and Spanish as she did so. I watched her carefully and enjoyed the ride, the visual and her wet snugness.

I ignored my vibrating pants again.

Gaaaaad! Thanks, Malcolm!

Carmen must've busted a nut a minimum of three times. I should have charged her ass. Anyway, she kissed me hard then led me back to the main area. I heard loud applause and cheering as we walked the hallway back to our table.

"What's with the cheering Carmen," I asked.

"Sugar," she announced, more irritated than I would have expected.

"Sugar," I repeated. Obviously whoever this Sugar was, she wasn't on Carmen's best friends list, more like she was on her shit list.

I made it back to the table, taking a seat that offered me a clear path to see the stage. Malcolm hadn't come back with Benzi yet, figured he was enjoying the same treatment I had received from Carmen with his chosen wench. Yes, I would definitely have to start coming here a bit more often, maybe even try to get a security gig.

Then, with the suddenness of a heart attack, I saw perfection. My eyes landed on the stage. What I saw prompted my mouth to hang open in awe. I saw the reason behind all the whooping and hollering floating across the stage. Fuck! She was the epitome of the purest form of desire, sex in its rawest incarnation. It looked like she sweated sex as she walked across the stage. She wore a white mask that was decorated in what looked to be some type of light- capturing studs, some colorful feathers flaring out from it as well. Her eyes where white! They were white with the darkest of black pupils centered in the middle of irises, which she used to hypnotize whatever creature she chose to place them on.(Had to be contacts.) Her hair was long, also white, with long black streaks running through it. If someone else attempted to wear these obvious props, they would appear to be in costume, but somehow these extras complemented her features to perfection. They added, rather than detracted or drew attention away from her considerable assets. Her skin was the color of rich vanilla pudding with a hint of cinnamon. I watched perfection gyrate to the music Deke played and got rock hard again instantly.

Carmen, who had her hand resting on my private area, instantly reacted to my arousal. "Fuck you, Papi," she yelled, then stormed away.

Women…

I continued to stare Sugar down from head to toe, joining everyone else in the establishment in worshiping at her altar. Before I knew it, I had my wallet out, twenties dangling to entice her to come closer. Sugar! Damn!

She made eye contact with me. I took in the sparkles. Wait, they were damn sugar crystals covering that already edible body. I licked my lips, started undulating my tongue. Wanted her to see I would eat her fucking ass out if she let me, right then and there, in front of everyone! I paused, shook my head vigorously. What the hell was I thinking?

I wondered if Sugar had cast a spell on us 'cause when I noticed the rest of the crowd, they were all in a sort of mesmerized state, damn near in a trance.

Sugar must have noticed my erotic tongue display and must've approved. She shimmied her body my way, swayed her African hips to and fro. Lovely! I took in her fair skin tone, found my way to her eyes, got lost in them for a second. Though her mask covered it, I could still ascertain Sugar was a blessed woman in the looks department as well as the body. The feathers of the mask flared outward, covered some of her cheeks, made her look even more exotic, even more mysterious.

I took a twenty, put it in my mouth so she could come take it. She smiled then, gave me her backside view. Sugar squatted, bent over and touched the floor, backed that sweet round mound right up to my face. She took my twenty. Grabbed it with clenching ass cheeks. Damn!

The crowd cheered. I barely heard them, was so into this vision of sin writhing in my face. After placing the twenty in the string of her G, Sugar backed her beautiful bottom up to my face again, left it there. Then she danced, danced the dance of the wanton, the sexual free, the Liliths, made her hips do circles and figure eights. My face was covered with ass! Sweet- smelling ass. Her kitty had a fruity taste. Yeah, that's right, I said taste!

I stuck my tongue all the way in Sugar. I gave her pussy the real "lap" dance. Sugar held her position while I flicked her clit and explored her honey pot, could tell she was loving it, 'cause she creamed my mouth with her tangy-tasting juices of pleasure. Then suddenly, without warning, she broke the connection, left me wanting more. Sugar turned, gave me a wicked grin, snatched my twenties and stuck them in her G-string. She then moved down the line to the next hard dick up in there but never broke eye contact with me, never broke that connection as she did so.

Damn!

"Wait!" I screamed. I fell over a couple of patrons, stumbling to get to her. Obviously, I drew the ire of some of the bouncers working and they moved to intercept me. I felt a hand on my shoulder, turned and found myself facing a smiling Malcolm.

"Relax, bro. She'll circle back around," he said.

I immediately calmed myself, knew I must look like a crazed drunken fool, but damn, Sugar had me all worked up. I could still taste her flavor on my tongue.

"What's gotten into your ass, Samp? You've been to strip clubs before, man."

"Yeah, but I ain't never seen a kitty cat like that," I said gesturing Sugar's way.

I noticed Mal taking in Sugar with his eyes then. Saw his current conquest storm off the same way Carmen had. Must be some serious jealousy floating around between the dancers. Mal studied Sugar like she was familiar to him. Somehow that possibility fostered a growing envy, a resentment in me. Damn, did he have to have all the fine-ass women around here!

Malcolm reached into his pocket, pulled out 10 crisp $100 bills, started waving them in the air, successfully gaining Sugar's and everyone else in the club's attention. Like a moth drawn to a flame, Sugar descended onto Malcolm. She kept her backside to him, thought she would repeat the same move on him that she had with me. Instead, she twerked that fine over-developed ass right in his face, twisted and rolled it at a fast pace like one of those Hawaiian hula dancers. I wanted to bust. Malcolm just played it cool as only he could do, sat back and acted nonchalant while this sexual seductress put on a show for him and the horny surrounding crowd.

Mal turned my way and smiled, gave me a few of the hundreds, then eased his hands around Sugars hips.

Not one bouncer moved to stop him!

Really!

I looked at the money in my hand and for some unknown reason, it came to represent disrespect in the highest form to me. I crumpled the bills up and threw them back in Mal's very surprised face. "You think I need your goddamn money, Mal? Why you always gotta flaunt your shit in everybody's faces…huh?"

"Samp,"

"No. Mal—ain't nobody ask you for shit!"

"You're drunk, man. Calm down. I know you're under a lot of stress lately. Just wanted you to have a good time is all, man."

"I was having a good fucking time, nigga, before you

started flaunting your bills. And what do you know about stress or what tha fuck I'm going through anyway!"

"I know a little about the investigation you're under, bro," he said. "Knew Jones was a good man and it must be hard for you to…"

"Shut the fuck up, Mal! You don't know shit! Don't worry about my problems. Worry about your own."

He asked, "My own?"

"Yeah Mal, like that whore-ass wife of yours. You know she back in Durham now and half of Durham is probably back in her."

Mal's demeanor shifted instantly. Bingo! I had hit the nerve, had found his kryptonite. Malcolm's eyes flashed with insane malice. I saw a promise of reprisal there, actually thought for a split second he was entertaining charging me and battling. Malcolm was not an extremely large man, but he was well over six feet and at least 220 pounds of muscled fury. Still, I prepared myself mentally for war.

"Samp!" Deke yelled. "That shit ain't right, man." Deke appeared and placed his body between Malcolm and me. I could see the hurt in his eyes. We were family, to Deke even more so, and I had crossed the line big time.

I lowered my head in disgust, felt my shoulders slump. Malcolm, I realized wasn't flaunting his money or his status, he was sharing, was simply sharing with his brother.

"My bad, Mal. I'm sorry, bro. Guess I've had a bit too much to drink, and I'm tripping."

Mal stared a hole through me, relaxed suddenly. "It's cool, Samp. I know we good, but keep my wife out your damn mouth like I kept your mama out of mine last night. I just gave her the dick." He grinned.

"Yeah, OK, but tell yours to stop texting me. " I laughed. "She keeps asking for this snake to come over and visit."

We both laughed, gave each other a man hug, held it for longer than the norm.

Situation dissolved.

Through all of the commotion, Sugar must have slipped away because we didn't see her for the rest of the night. Guess she had more important things to attend to. I made a mental promise to get me some Sugar, wanted it before my boys got to it.

Deke   6

I don't know what was up between Samp and Mal the other night at the club, but it looked to be pretty intense. I just hope they get it together. I needed us to be in a good place if we were going to be business partners. They would be silent partners, but we still needed to be able to work together. From what I could discern, Sugar had Sample's nose wide open. I hope that wasn't the case though, 'cause I knew how territorial Samp can be over some ass. If he only knew I already had a taste of Sugar and was planning on going back for another.

Sugar, like her name, was a damn drug, like a narcotic, addictive as hell. At least I had the good sense to recognize that. After our little sexcapade the other night, I had concluded, Sugar was a stone-cold freak and definitely not a one-man woman. Shit, she was probably a switch hitter as well, loving cats as well as dogs. I smiled. It was all good to me cause I wasn't' looking to marry her, just wanted to make money with her. The sex was just a bonus. It somewhat troubled me, though. The whole time we were "sweating to the oldies," I kept thinking this was too good to be true yet halfway through, the mask, contacts, and hair started to creep me out a little. Sugar never ever took off those props. She would strategically maneuver my hands so I wouldn't come near her face. I wondered who she was underneath the disguise. Wondered, not for the first time, if I knew her from somewhere. She seemed very familiar to me at times but then it would fade. I still couldn't place that banging-ass body and the sultry voice.

Sugar…her sexuality haunts me, though. I am uneasy in her presence at times. Lying with her is almost like having a python as a pet. Sure you can cuddle with it if you want. It will wrap its body around yours, only you never know if it's for companionship or predatory purposes. You never know when you may be its prey, but you understand that if you're not careful, you eventually will be. That is Sugar in a nutshell.

Anyway, thanks to Malcolm, I had finally gotten my '79 Impala back on the road, was on my way to Southpoint Mall to do a little window shopping and have an impromptu business meeting via cell phone with Black. One of his lackeys was supposed to meet me at Champs. Damn. Black is always with this covert shit. He always had been a paranoid soul who didn't trust a muthafucca, which made him do things differently. That was probably why it was so hard for Durham's finest to get charges to stick to him. The only reason he was doing a six- month stint now was for probation violation.

Black had caught Kesha, his baby mama, with some nigga from the West End at one of the four houses he owned. He had the poor fool beaten within an inch of his life and he himself went Mayweather on Kesha. Obviously he went too far, 'cause he knocked out some of lovely Kesha's front teeth. Needless to say, the female district attorney frowns on such actions and revoked his probation even though Kesha's scared devoted ass wouldn't press charges. Shit, she was still fine as hell, even with her missing fangs, snaggletooth bitch. One just didn't cross Black.

I just hoped word hadn't found its way to his ears about me fucking Sugar. I didn't know what their relationship was, and I didn't need Black pissed with me just yet.

Malcolm and Sampson were still considering my offer, and I had to put a helluva business plan together for Mal to sink his teeth into. He would be the primary investor after all. I guess those business management courses I took in college were finally going to come in handy. I was putting in major hours with this proposal. I could see my world changing for the better if I could secure this partnership with my boys.

I looked up from nursing the cup of frozen yogurt I had gotten when I arrived at the food court to see perfection walking my way.

She should have been mine, being the one who stayed on my mind constantly.

My Eve.

"Hey, Deke," Rochelle said.

I nodded. Tried to keep my voice steady, keep the

trembling out. "Rochelle," I managed.

There she was in all her glory. Rochelle, my best friend's wife, the woman I had eyes for first but had lost out to my brother. I had dated her before Malcolm. She had cheated on me with him, gotten pregnant, and chose him.

She was still as fine as ever, still beautiful in every way.

Rochelle was a classic beauty, never needed makeup, though I could tell money agreed with her. She now looked like an expensive piece of ass. She was decked out in one of those business-type suits for women, the ones with a skirt instead of pants. It was grey in color. She accentuated it with an expensive-looking white blouse, a blouse that brought new meaning to the word cleavage. The outfit looked like it was molded to her body, showed all of her "slap yo' mama" curves.

I couldn't help but stare at her toned legs as she walked toward me. Damn those high heels!

Rochelle's hair was cropped in a short but elegant style, looked great on her head, appeared as though it cost a grip to maintain. I kept scanning her from head to toe, my eyes lingering on her ample breasts, then her beautiful face.

"You taking a picture, Deke," she laughed. That sound instantly stimulated my lower region.

"Oh—no. Ro, just good to see you is all."

"Uh-huh…"

"I asked Mal about you the other night," I said.

"Yeah, I just bet you did," she grinned. "You still looking good, Deke. Heard you were getting yourself together, too. Got you a legit job and everything."

"That's right," I said, a little puzzled.

"That's good, Deke. That's real good. Black likes you, so don't go fucking this up, OK?" Vulgarity looked blasphemous coming from her beautiful lips but also seemed sexy as well.

"How you know about me and Black?" I asked.

"Went to see him the other day. You know he is like my brother, considering we practically grew up in the same household. We always stay in touch. He keeps me informed on what's going on in the Bull City.

I took in her regal appearance again, tried to picture her slumming at the jailhouse with convicts, no doubt salivating at her beautiful image. Rochelle was always Rochelle, no matter how much money Malcolm and she had. Ro always kept it real.

"So you asked Black about me, huh?" I inquired. "Why would you trouble yourself with what's happening in my pathetic life? You made your choice years ago. Looks like you made the right one for your family. Malcolm is a better husband and provider than I ever would have been."

"Deke, please don't. Don't sell yourself short. I know you loved me with all you had. I cared for you as well, still do, but I had to make a decision that was in the best interest for me and my unborn twins at the time."

"Ro—"

"No Deke, listen to me for a minute. Malcolm got me pregnant, remember. I know I shouldn't have fucked your best friend while I was your woman, but things happen. He wanted me in a way you didn't. He had plans, was going places, and wanted me by his side and made it a point to share all his plans for us with me."

"Rochelle, I know all of this. Mal is like my brother. I got over the two of you being together a long time ago, was at the wedding, remember? Believe it or not, if I had to lose you to someone, Mal would be my choice."

"Really," she said. There was a level of skepticism in her voice.

"Yes, Ro, really. I'm just glad you are happy."

"Happy?"

"Yeah, happy," I stated.

"I wouldn't quite say all that, but I am satisfied. Malcolm provides me and the boys with a good stable life. He is a good father as well. The bastard just can't keep his dick in his pants when I'm not around." She inhaled then exhaled deeply.

"I'm tired of it, Dee." She used her pet name for me. "Maybe I need to get me some Strange."

"Oh?" My eyes met hers. She was speaking to me without using words now, making me an offer, an offer I couldn't take but wouldn't refuse.

Rochelle placed her hand on my knee, leaned in close enough for me to inhale her scent.

"I got this itch that I need to scratch, Dee," she breathed into my ear.

I instantly started to swell, couldn't help but respond in that manner. I immediately became drunk with her smell, started to lean in, going for those luscious lips.

Then her cell rang. Damn!

"Hello, oh, yes I'll accept the charges. Hey, Black. Yes, he's here. Hold on, OK?"

Rochelle handed me the phone letting her hand roam up

my thigh as she did so. She grabbed a handful, smiled, then got up and walked deeper into the mall.

I along with a few other men (and women) watched her fine backside as she strutted, wondered what it looked like naked now. She was a bit thicker and more toned than she was when I had savored her treats in my bed years ago. Those days, she was just a girl. Now shit. Rochelle was all woman, beautiful woman. I would just love to take a drive down her curvy lanes. I smiled to myself, maybe I would.

"Deke!" Black shouted in the phone.

"Oh, what up, Black? What's going on?"

"Nothing but time, little cuz. Run my numbers from the week to me 'cause I got a lot of shit to take care of today."

Black was all business, as usual. I knew the routine by now, though. One would think I was the manager at the club, but Black trusted me to recite the books to him weekly, me and only me.

I sighed, looked the way Rochelle had walked, conjured up the image of that ass again in my mind, pulled out my notepad, and began to give my weekly report.

Sampson   7

I clicked on the flat screen in my den and bam! "Durham police officer Rodney Rico Sampson was placed on unpaid suspension following investigations of his possible involvement in the unsolved death of his former partner." That damn bitch-ass reporter seemed happy to give that news to the public. Bitch! "Detective Steven L. Jones was a stalwart in the community and he leaves behind a pregnant wife and child from a previous relationship. Police Captain Tony Davis vows to solve this crime turning over as many stones as need be. We will have more coverage at 11."

Damn!

Motherfuckers suspended my ass and it was all over the fucking morning news. Shit, I just got the word last night! My phone had been ringing off the hook since that shit first aired this morning The damn niggas I had been shaking down were calling, threatening my ass and I couldn't do shit about it. Watts had pulled a disappearing act at the time I needed her the most, and I kept seeing black SUVs in my neighborhood on the regular. They were really on my ass about Jonesy. I didn't kill him, shit! Sure, I had left him on that dead-in street to get ambushed, but it was Black that wanted him dead. I knew his murder would benefit me as well though. Jonesy was on to me and would have gone to Internal Affairs sooner or later. He had given me a chance to turn myself in. Fuck that! He had to go...

I'm just glad I had decided to invest in Deke's idea for the club when I did because that income was helping to pay my bills now. Those I.A. fucks had frozen my bank accounts, something about possible payoffs I was taking, so all I had was what cash I had stashed at the crib and the profits from club Sugarland. It had taken about 2 months to get it up and running.

Sugarland! I had come up with the name. It fit, considering Sugar was our money maker and headliner. We had been open for business about three weeks now, and business was booming. Sugar had even gone back to Georgia, had convinced some of her friends in the business to come up and work our club, for a finder's fee ,of course. All this happened very quickly once Malcolm agreed to be the main financier, and I chipped in with some of my own savings. Just like Deke had promised, the club was a damn goldmine.

Sugarland itself looked to be a nice upscale spot for everyone from the local businessman, to the average Joe Blow with a 9 to 5, to that pharmaceutical street businessman with cash aplenty. They all congregated to it.

We spared little expense in the building and decorating of the club. Everything was new and state of the art, from the sound system to the high-definition flat screens, strategically placed around the club. Hell, even the dancers had first class dressing rooms, which they all loved. We went for the upscale look and feel but still had that anything-goes atmosphere of the hole-in-the wall clubs. Shit, in just a few weeks, Sugarland was the talk of the south. Hello!

Fuck the DPD! I was in love with the perks of being a successful club owner. I still hadn't been able to corner Sugar just yet. Each night she managed to slip through my grasp, but I was determined more than ever to bed that wench. Shit, I had my suspicions of who the masked bitch with the seductive moves was really anyway. I couldn't believe no one had figured it out. Yes, she wore the masks, the hair, and the contacts, but that body, those moves, that confident ass strut. It had to be who I suspected. The skin tone was almost a match. It had to be her.

Black had word sent to me that he wanted a meeting; I hadn't seen or spoken to him since the opening of Sugarland. It had to be about the club. Black couldn't be happy Sugar left his shack and came to work for us, but I wondered why it had taken this long for him to come a calling. Figured he'd talk to me before he talked to Deke anyway.

I was on my way to the jailhouse, about to pull out of my driveway when a Durham City patrol car pulled in behind my vehicle.

Fuck, now what?

She exited the car and I smiled.

"What's up, Watts? Where you been?"

"Told you my mother was sick weeks ago, Sample. You don't listen, you big lunkhead. I had to go to Georgia and take care of her and things for a while."

"Oh, my bad. How's she doing?"

Ignoring my question of concern, she asked, "Where are you off to?"

I said, "Got a meeting to attend."

"So what you gonna do, baby. I heard they got your big dick in a sling," she smirked. "Did you do it, Samp? Did you have Jonesy killed?"

I looked Watts up and down. Could tell she had been stressed as of late, looked like she had dropped 10 pounds.

"You wearing a wire Watts," I stated more than questioned.

"Really, Sample…a wire? You really believe I would wear a wire for them?" She honestly looked hurt. "I've had other shit on my plate, OK? I'm sorry I haven't been here for you, but I'm here now. Only you have to keep it real with me because I understand full well you are no angel. My eyes are wide open, Samp."

"Yeah, I'm no saint, but I didn't have anything to do with Jonesy being offed."

"OK, baby, that's good enough for me." She sounded relieved, moved to hug me.

"I gotta go, Watts, but can I get up with you later tonight."

"Where? At club Sugarland?" she said. "Yeah, Samp, I know about your new whore house. When were you planning on telling me you got a stable of bitches now?"

"Now, Watts . . .,"

"Save it, Sample. Just meet me here at around midnight 'cause I got some stress to get rid of. I need my back cracked." She grinned devilishly. "Can you at least handle that for me?"

"You just wait and see, babe."

With that Watts leaned in, tongued the shit out of me, and licked all over my lips, as if she were tasting and savoring my natural flavor.

"Hmmmm…you taste good. See you later, player."

I watched her ass twist to and fro in those tight-ass police-issued pants from my rearview mirror. Damn, Watts was back. I had to figure out where I wanted her to fit into my life now.

As I started to pull out, another black-on-black truck came cruising down my street. It never stopped, but I knew they were there to fuck with me.

Bastards!

$ $ $

My trip downtown was uneventful, didn't see any black trucks in my rear. I walked into the jailhouse without any confrontations, entered the visiting area with Black already waiting for me.

"Officer Sample. Oops, my bad. That should be former officer now, isn't it?"

"What the hell do you want, Black? I ain't got time for

this shit now."

"Make time, nigga, cause you owe me, Samp, remember?"

I took in Black's appearance. Even in those ridiculous-looking orange jumpsuits, he was intimidating. Black was about 6'8" around 350 bills, most of it muscle. He combined that imposing physical stature with an extremely bad temper. A bad combo for a big man, cause his crazy ass was always in trouble with the law for one thing or the other. He used to beat up grown-ass men when he was 12!

Black was a bad child, who turned into a terrible teen, who then became an even worse adult. Look up thug in the dictionary and you would find his insane ass smiling back at you. I was no small man myself, but even I, nor any other sane person with good sense, messed with this menace to society. But he was caged now, so fuck 'em!

"OK, Black, what's this all about," I asked in an even tone.

"Sugarland, Sample. It's all about Sugarland. Word on the street is you niggas are jammed packed every night."

"So?"

"So, muthafucka, I think it's time we figure out my cut since I supplied the Sugar in Sugar-land." He let an evil smile creep across his face as he spoke. "It's only fair, don't you think?"

"Look, Black, you don't own Sugar. She is a legal citizen of these United States as far as I know, so she has the right to work wherever she damn well pleases."

"Check your tone, nigga, before I check you into a room at Scarborough," he said referring to a local black funeral home.

"Black, you don't scare me," I lied. "Make all the threats you want but you ain't doing shit to me or my boys behind these bars. I heard they bout to get your hood ass for conspiracy anyway. So worry about not dropping the soap, nigga."

"Oh, you bold now, huh? You grown a set, Samp." He was practically spitting with every syllable he spoke. His saliva dripped down the glass barrier that was between us. I could almost detect steam rising off his bald head, his anger had risen so. "I'll have your nuts fed to my dogs, nigga!" He was shouting now, drawing unwanted attention our way.

"Cool it, Black." That came from one of the armed guards on his side of the glass.

Black's scowl instantly transformed into a menacing grin, looked like a serpent about to strike its prey.

"I'm good," he said to the guard. "Now, Sample." His tone was sweet but had the edge of a butcher's knife." Don't force me into an uncomfortable position. Please. I already got to deal with Deke. I was quite fond of him, but he used me it would seem. I know you two are like brothers or lovers or whatever, but surely it would be in your best interest to just pay me what I'm owed."

"And that is?"

"Forty percent of the weekly take," he continued to sport the predatory smile.

I yelled, "Forty percent! Nigga, are you crazy!"

"It's a small price to pay if you ask me,' cause I could just take it all or burn your shit to the ground. This way, at least, everybody gets a little something."

"Communicating threats, Black. Temper, temper. That could bring you another unwanted charge."

Black stood then, let his massive bulk do his talking for him a bit. He held eye contact with me for effect. "I can get to you, Sample," he calmly stated. "I can get to all of you."

"So you say, Blackwell. I ain't on your payroll anymore so you can go to hell and as far as those threats of yours are concerned, nigga. I stay strapped, too."

He smiled. "You just a crooked-ass cop, Samp. There are ways to deal with you."

"Haven't you heard, Black, they took my fucking badge."

"Yeah, I heard, nigga. You a goddamn fool too, cause your ignorant ass don't even realize that badge is what kept your leeching ass alive and above ground in the streets." He leaned in closer to the barrier then and whispered. "Without it, how long do you think your life expectancy is now? Huh?"

I got up then, walked out. I was a little shaken by that last statement. I should maybe have handled that confrontation differently, should have censored my mouth, was too late now. What was done was done. One thing for sure, I was going to have to explain this predicament to Malcolm and Deke.

As I walked to my car, I saw her approaching my way, strolling in her usual jaw-dropping gait. She wore a tight-fitting outfit with an accompanying tight smug look on her face once her eyes fell on me.

"Hello, Rochelle," I said, as if her name were profanity.

"Hello, Simple…ah…I mean, Sample. Funny seeing you here. I guess you getting ready for your new home," she said.

"Yeah, well it's always good to see your ghetto ass, too, Ro."

Rochelle eyeballed me with total disdain etched on her beautiful fucking face. The bitch hated my guts, and I have to say it was more than mutual. You see, she was still upset with me for making her cum like a fountain in front of her husband and only she and I knew the truth of it. I stuck out my tongue, undulated it her way, made it dance serpentine. She stared, could read recollection in her face. I grinned at her physical response.

"Bet your panties are soaked just thinking 'bout how I ate your pretty ass out that time."

"Fuck you! It will never happen again, pig! Oh, that's right. I can't call you that anymore. Bastard!"

She pushed past me, and I turned to watch that phat ass twist and shout in that skirt as she strutted up the walkway. Damn! Yeah, I had seen all that before, that shimmy and shake. I began to reminisce about our once-in-a lifetime chance encounter, the encounter that shouldn't have happened, but did. I knew what my good friend's wife tasted like, what she felt like, and we both kept it our dirty little secret. Though sometimes, I wondered if Mal ever put two and two together.

It happened about five years ago. I was dating this freak named Janet I had met off of one of those African-American dating websites. She was into threesomes and swinging parties. That chick turned me on to a lot of madness. She took me to this invitation-only party in Virginia, think we were just outside of Richmond.

It was in this well-to-do gated community, looked like the hosts were loaded. When we entered the place, all I saw were barely clothed men and women wearing masks socializing with one another. The house had four levels. We entered in on the second. It had an open floor plan so it easily accommodated about 20 couples or so in the main sparsely furnished entertainment room. It was decorated in high-tech to modern furniture and electronics. They had some weird-ass music wafting through the house, as well. The place was dimly lit with candlelight, and what I managed to see by its illumination was pretty much a sexual free for all.

People were engaging in threesomes, foursomes, damn near any-somes. There were thick, expensive-looking blankets spread across the hardwood floors with bodies lying atop them, writhing this way and that. I guessed blacks, whites, Asians, and Latinos were all represented in a multiracial sexual dance that I was witnessing, as well as large, skinny, muscular, and voluptuous bodies being fucked with little regard to who watched.

Janet, my…uh…date… immediately stripped and joined two black men and a full-figured Caucasian woman on the floor, just blended right in with them.

I still remained clothed for awhile and decided to do some exploring of the house. I found a multitude of bedrooms, each decorated with different themes. There was a moon theme, a tropical theme. I stopped at the winter theme that I encountered.

The room was adorned with blue lights and fake snowflakes with mock ice crystals hanging from the ceiling. The air was very cold in this room. There was a transparent glass door with frost collecting on it that added a more chilly effect to the room. I took a peek in and saw two women going at it savagely.

One had her head buried in the other's southern comfort, had her hands behind the prone woman's knees, so the woman getting pleased was stretched wide for maximum pleasure. The woman doing the pleasing was bobbing her head up and down vigorously, had a deceptively long tongue that she was putting to good use.

I was enthralled by this woman. She reminded me of my boy's wife, Rochelle, but it couldn't be her, not with her Bible-toting self.

I had seen Rochelle naked once when I had stayed with her and Mal, visiting them one weekend. She was conveniently coming out of the shower, and I was looking for a towel. Rochelle didn't even flinch, didn't try to cover herself. She just lingered in the doorway giving me an extended look. I remember finding it difficult to swallow as I took in her exposed flesh, probably drooled a little, too. She just stood and stared at my growing crotch, stared and smiled. I believe she wanted me to make a move. When none came, she immediately became irate and has treated me like stir fried shit ever since.

I always kept a mental Polaroid of her incredible body in my consciousness, and this woman's frame was strangely similar.

The two women were completely nude save for the

masks they wore. I had adorned a half- covering face mask myself, its ivory-white hue contrasted with my coal-black skin tone.

I entered the room, and they both looked up briefly, making gestures for me to join them. I could barely make out their ethnicities because of the eerie blue light, but it highlighted their curves just perfectly.

The one who reminded me of Rochelle moved to disrobe me. I let her free my master from my pants and start to stroke him slow. She moaned as she did so. Number two's hands were between her thighs as well. Two came up to me and began to lick my balls in unison with one's stroking. I grew even more. Rochelle's doppelganger gasped at my length, she put both hands around me and worked me over that way for a while, pushed me on my back on the large bed that was in the room.

Number two got up, kissed the head my dick, and told the other, "Enjoy girlfriend, he's way too big for my little punani. I ain't even trying to handle all that meat."

The twin smiled and said, "Good, more for me. I like things that cum in big packages." I was so worked up by this time. I was hard as nails and I wanted to nail something but first I decided to prep her just right. I flipped her over on her back, pinned her down, and spread her legs out wide, dove in head first, tongue flickering. She tasted sweet... so fruity... so damn good. I started exploring every inch, every crevice of her southpark. My hands worked her clit while my tongue backed them up.

She wailed like a banshee, came all over my face, just kept gushing. Her explosion hit her with such force that she knocked her own damn mask off. I couldn't help but see who I had been feasting on. It was indeed Rochelle! She was so satisfied that she didn't even try to put the mask back on, just lay there breathing heavy.

"You've seen mine, now can I see yours," she had said to me." I hesitated, was prepared to just show her it was me, but as luck would have it, Malcolm came into the room then and saved the day.

Apparently, he had been watching at the door while receiving some serious fellatio from the chick who had left us alone. He stormed in talking about the rules of the house and practically ordered Rochelle to put her mask back on. He never even recognized me, probably due to that eerie blue light. But he had witnessed me giving his wife an Earth-shattering orgasm, and never knew it was one of his best friends doing it.

I just slipped out while they were, ah discussing the issue, found Janet, and piledrived her thick ass right there in front of everyone to the applause of many. Then we left and got a hotel room in downtown Richmond to continue our night of fornicating.

A few months after that incident, Mal and Rochelle were in town attending a barbeque at my house. Rochelle was being, well, Rochelle toward me, and I couldn't resist it, so I spilled the beans to put her in her place. She actually acted as if it wasn't that big of a surprise, but I could tell I had her spooked. She didn't want her freaky lifestyle getting out to her Bible-toting family. So she just denied it and became even bitchier toward me, but we both knew the truth.

I had tamed that phat wild ass and made her have a squirting orgasm. All this flashed through my mind as Rochelle pushed past me. "Been wearing any masks lately," I said.

She turned my way. "What? Hell no, Simple. I don't need masks when I'm home but you might, 'cause word on the street is niggas gunning for you. Goodbye, Simple."

"Whatever, Ro, see you at the club."

"It will be a cold day in hell before I set foot in y'all's den of sin. I got better things to do with my time, but you continue to pack the place, to make that money for me to spend, fool."

I gave her a one -finger salute then walked to my car. As I pulled out, a black-on-black SUV cruised by purposefully slow.

Fuck!

Malcolm   8

I had sat there for a few minutes, watching the exchange between Rochelle and Sampson. I had taken an early lunch, wanted to surprise my wife at home with some lunchtime frisky business, but I had seen her candy-apple red convertible Mercedes race down a busy Duke Street as I exited 15-501. I took a right rather than my usual left and followed her. I stayed back far enough as to not be spotted and she eventually led me to the downtown Durham area, specifically the county jailhouse.

Their interaction was as cold as ever from what I could ascertain. Got me to thinking that they reminded me of two jilted old lovers. I didn't know why they hated each other so, but I made a mental note to find out.

Rochelle looked too damn good, so mouth-watering edible as she sashayed past Sample and made that ample ass roll to her own internal beat, prompting everyone around to stare, to lock eyes on that magnificent behind and no doubt fantasize about what she was like in the sack. I knew. I understood.

I smiled, then frowned, pleased she was my wife but displeased where she had led me to. She was obviously here to see that miserable excuse of family, her cousin Blackwell.

I never really cared much for my wife's relationship with this psychopathic family member. As far as I was concerned, he was half the reason for some of her amoral past. A past she kept hidden from her mother and scripture-quoting preacher father, kept it secret from most of her relatives in the country. They didn't know the type of girl Rochelle had become when she left Mebane and went to live with Black's people, in Durham, when she was 14 or 15. She was wide open wild.

In those days, Black opened up a barbershop off of Alston Avenue, looked like an abandoned house that he fixed up, but he shrewdly obtained some of the best barbers in town. I remember everybody went to Black's to get a haircut then.

Black, to his credit, was always thinking of ways to make money. I seem to recall on Fridays, he would close down the shop and turn it into a—how should I say— bootleg strip club with teenage girls and young women from the surrounding neighborhoods, applying their chosen trade.

Sample and myself played basketball for Northern High, while Deke was a point guard for Hillside. We all played for Black in the summer, though, played for his championship city league team. Black was the one who had given us our nickname "The Triplets." Being on his team definitely had its perks. One of which was free haircuts at his barbershop, so we were always there.

That's where I first laid love-clouded eyes on Rochelle. Rochelle, the pretty little girl with the phat ass who worked the register at Black's barbershop, the beauty who always had a smile and conversation for me at every visit. Only problem was Deke, my brotha, had eyes for her as well, and he was faster on the draw than I was in those days. Deke had always been a smooth talker with the ladies, and he wasted no time in gaining Rochelle's favor with his gift of gab. By the time I gathered up my nerve to ask her out, Deke had already secured her affections, and once I realized that, I resigned myself to pining for her from afar. Besides, Black stood ever watchful over his little cousin, and you had to have his blessing, or else.

The fact that Black and Rochelle were more like brother and sister than cousins by marriage kept a lot of potential suitors away.

Black's father had married her aunt, so that's how she came to live with them. She wanted to attend school in Durham so her holier-than-thou parents agreed to let her attend the Science & Math Academy, never knowing what they were unleashing on the city—the preacher's daughter.

Hell, everyone I knew fantasized about Rochelle Johnson, but Deke got to her first. He brought her stuff at every barber visit. Shoot, Deke brought flowers, candy, jewelry—hell, he even brought the girl a two piece from Church's Chicken every other day.

I asked her once why did she get with Deke before me.

She stated simply that he had worn her down, that he was cute and I was playing it too cool so she had to do something to make me make a move. Rochelle had had eyes for me all along, but I didn't want to cross the line between her and Deke.

Until…

There came a Friday where we were all drinking heavily at Black's. Deke had gone on a recruiting trip to Prairie View College. They wanted him desperately to be their starting point guard. Black had been caught with a couple of ounces of weed in his truck earlier that day, but he let Rochelle open up the spot for Friday night fun anyway.

It was a "bring your own bottle" type of joint, so I had copped a half gallon of Absolute. Rochelle and I were chilling in one of the back rooms getting straight shit faced. Evidently, I passed out back there trying to hang, and when I came to, there was whooping and hollering, clapping and whistling.

I didn't think it was strange because, like I said, several around-the-way chicks would come over and strip to make some extra bills on Fridays. I got up, head was kind of spinning, stumbled to the front room where I heard the commotion.

That's when I saw what I saw.

She was in the middle of the room twerking that ass with a partner; both dropping it like it's hot. Rochelle had taken her shirt and skirt off. She was in a lacy black bra and matching thong, didn't leave much to the imagination, unless you imagined freaky shit. Her dance partner was the younger, chunkier girl who lived a couple of houses down from Black's parents' house. She was cute as well, just thick in a baby fat kind of way. She wore nothing but some tight-ass Daisy Duke shorts cutting into her soft flesh. It looked to me that Rochelle was drunk, but her counterpart was the same plus high as a kite. She didn't seem to even notice that her large breasts were flopping to and fro with every dance move she executed.

Then I saw Sample standing to the side, his shirt off, burning blunt dangling in his mouth. He smirked at me as I gawked at Rochelle. Sample came up on the other girl then, gyrated behind her as he palmed her breasts, which continued to mirror a shaking bowl of Jell-O. He grabbed her waist, spun her around till she faced him and gave her a long-lasting shotgun blast of chronic that looked like it went straight to her head and G-spot. The girl cocked one thick curvy leg on Samp's shoulder and danced wickedly sexual on him. The other guys in the room applauded and cheered her on.

Rochelle, to her credit, was not about to be out done. She grinded her way over to Sample and made her butt cheeks dance to the rhythm of the lewd hip hop song blaring in the room. I watched, hypnotized by her swaying hips and jiggling ass. Samp went to grab her as well. That's when I came out of my stupor and rushed in to pull her out of there. Before I could execute my foggy plan, though, the cute chunky girl intercepted me, put her prematurely well-developed boobs in my face then slithered her body lower down mine, started simulating oral pleasure on my crotch.

The look on Rochelle's face could have killed bunny

rabbits. She stormed over, pushed the girl on her back, grabbed my hand, snatched some money that had been thrown on the floor, and led me out of the house. She pulled on her shirt and skirt once we got to the front porch.

"What was that all about, Ro," I asked.

"Shut the…shhh…shut the fuck up and come here," she slurred.

I stood in front of Rochelle. She grabbed my crotch forcefully then pulled me in and tongued the hell out of me. We stayed like that for what seemed like hours but was more like seconds.

"Let's go get a room, Mal."

"A room?"

"Yeah, a room. You know, where one goes to fuck." She held up the cash she had swiped from the floor. "My treat," she said.

"What about Deke, Rochelle?" I asked, not really wanting the answer.

"What about him?" Rochelle gave me this look of pure unadulterated lust then took my hand and placed it in the fire raging between her thighs so I could feel her humidity. "Are you really going to turn this down?"

I tried to stall her a bit. "You really going to leave your girl in there by herself, Ro?" I asked.

"Fuck that bitch! She shouldn't have put her fat-ass hands on you!"

I was a little worried about the girl, now that I think about it, but the alcohol had killed my sense of responsibility. "Let's go." I stated before I lost my nerve.

As we were leaving, the yells and screams drifting from

the house grew even louder, sounded like a girl's voice was mixed in. I figured that the chunky girl must be in there making her money taking it all off by now. Then we saw Black pull up with his crew of felons. Rochelle waved. I was like, damn he must have some serious bank because he just got busted earlier in the day. I was also glad I had gotten Rochelle out of the stripping room before he arrived. That would have been an ugly scene had I not. I had seen Black punch guys in the face just for gawking at Rochelle's beauty at a distance. I could well imagine what he would have done had he seen his little sister in front of a crowd stripping.

We pulled up at the Cricket Inn on Hillindale. Classy, it was not, but a room was a room as far as I was concerned with both our hormones raging.

We fucked like rabbits all night long, used up every condom from the pack of twelve I purchased on the way over. It wasn't until the next morning when the alcohol had worn off, the condoms were all gone, and we were in bed naked and really talking, that we made love for the first time, unprotected.

It was slow, it was meaningful, it was beautiful, and as a result, she emerged from that lovemaking pregnant with our twins an exact nine months later. I grew up then, became a man and got serious about everything. To his credit, Deke forgave us and gave our wedding his blessing. I went to college a married man. Had graduated with Rochelle by my side the whole time. We were both determined to make a good life for our twins.

Deke   9

Sample had phoned to tell me about his meeting with Black. I knew it would come to this sooner or later, and sooner was my guess when that crazy mofo was involved. But in all my time dealing with Black, I had never seen his terrible anger aimed my way. Now I was sure I was in his crosshairs. The feeling was unsettling.

I had seen what being the object of Black's wrath could mean, knew full well what he could and would do to me if I fell completely out of his favor. Sample knew as well. I don't think Mal understood the magnitude of us hiring Sugar to build our club around.

But fucking 40 percent! Black must be smoking the shit he slanging!

Sugar had seemed nonchalant about the whole situation, like she was untouchable or something. She told me she had a telephone conversation with Black prior to joining Sugarland, and she intimated to me that Black gave her his blessing. I really didn't believe that shit, but I also didn't know the ins and outs of their relationship. Maybe he was so calm and understanding with her because he planned to take it out on my ass, Sample's and Mal's. For all I knew, he told Sugar to work for us so he could extort this outrageous sum of money later.

Black may be a thuggish psycho, but he is also a shrewd business man. A very little known fact about him was that his homicidal ass was an accomplished chess player, had picked it up in prison as I recall. He studied that game like he could use its lessons for living his life. Black began to orchestrate his business affairs like pieces on a chess board. To tell the truth, that way of thinking was why he had and kept Durham on lock.

I glanced at this week's figures as I drove to my new home. We were doing very well in each of the club's money makers, alcohol and the dancers being the largest. We had also expanded and had gambling machines in a side room that was starting to turn a significant profit as well.

There was no fucking way we were giving up 40 percent of our take. Hell, it was already split three ways with Malcolm receiving the largest portion.

I pulled into the driveway of my new house. Yes, house! When I got out of jail those many months ago, Black put me up in an apartment in Willowdale, right off of Guess Road near the Chinese joint with the bomb ass honey wings. It wasn't the hood by a long shot, but I figured it was time to step up my living arrangements, especially when we opened Sugarland. I had found a nice little spot in north Raleigh, off of 401, away from the madness of the Durham scene. I finally felt like I was succeeding in something once I signed the lease on the house. It was a quaint three bedroom, sitting on a half-acre of land, just perfect for me - a nice quiet spot.

As I pulled up, I saw my neighbor's kids playing in their front yard. I glanced in my rearview mirror and noticed a black-on-black SUV driving past my home. It looked a little like Sugar's truck.

That night, she had followed me to my place. She drove a dark truck with dark-ass tint. She didn't drive it all the time, though, but that night I took notice because the tint was so damn dark I couldn't see her sexy ass in the truck. It was either a Yukon or Tahoe, I think.

Something else occurred to me. Black was known for his black-on-black vehicles with the smoked-out tinted windows.

Instantly, my nerves were on edge, hands began to shake.

Damn! He knows where I live!

Malcolm 10

After following and spying on my wife, I returned to work. The rest of my day was uneventful. I received a call from Sampson informing me about Black's financial demands. Frankly, it made me laugh. Samp didn't seem to find humor in the situation, though. I could hear the stress in his voice as he spoke.

"This fool means business, Mal," he had stated with a quivering tone.

"Don't worry, bro. We can put our heads together and handle this problem," I returned. "I will call in some favors if I have to. I made a few acquaintances while in DC. Don't worry, man."

I told him that I'd probably see him later at Sugarland. To tell the truth, I had not been there much, was content to let Deke run things since this was his baby. I was pleased with my share of the profits. Deke was right. It was a goldmine!

I really wanted to see Sugar dance again, though. I hadn't really seen her since that night we all went to Black's little hole-in-the wall club. It was so dim in there, couldn't really see her too well anyway. She reminded me of someone, though. Her movements, had seen them before. I was sure of it. Sugar sported a distinctive tattoo on her inner thigh that I had noticed that night. It was a burning bird, a phoenix, I believe. The bird of revenge, the entity that wouldn't die. That tat had me curious. I didn't remember any of the women I had bedded having such a tattoo, but still she seemed familiar, masks and all.

I wanted to watch her again, more closely, maybe coax that mask off, maybe coax them panties off as well. I smiled. Yes, Sugar would not be an easy conquest. She was into her own thing, master of her crazy-ass world, struck me as the type who picked her lovers rather than being seduced. Sugar didn't play by others' rules. I liked that about her. Hell, the fact that she was employed where I had a part in ownership and I didn't even know her identity deserved kudos on her part. She definitely had piqued my curiosity. I was determined to crack her wall of mysteries, if Sampson and Deke didn't beat me to it.

I was well aware Deke had banged her, hat Samp was infatuated with her, but none of us really knew much about this sexy woman who had hundreds of men flocking to our club to see her strut her stuff. It unnerved me to say the least. She could be dangerous, in a fun kind of way, could be my Pandora's Box.

I tried to focus on my work then, my real j-o-b. It was still hours before I was due at the club anyway.

$ $ $

As I pulled my Jag into one of the three owner-designated parking spots, I glanced around the parking lot. It was filled to capacity as usual. Hell, some were even parking on a side street and footing the short walk over. I couldn't argue with what I saw. Business was definitely booming.

I nodded to Kevin and Devin, the twin linebacker-looking brutes we had hired for security of the club. They and their crew were extremely well worth the money. We had a lot of upscale clientele as well as regular working-class folk who all wanted to feel comfortable in an after-hours establishment. We provided that with the on-point security. Nothing, absolutely nothing, got by the twins.

I went straight to my office, had Simone, one of our lovely young bartenders, bring me a drink. She worked in a thong as well, and I patted her striking backside as she turned to leave.

"Maybe later, Mister Lee," she said, her thong riding between two gorgeous mounds the color of brown sugar.

"Simone…Simone…when are you going to try the stage, cause I know you'd make a killing on the pole."

"I don't know, Mister Lee, whenever I get the nerve, I guess. I could never feel as comfortable as Sugar or the other girls with all those men gawking at my goods, sexing me down with their leering eyes."

I looked at her bartending outfit. "Really, Simone, you're practically showing your goods now, not that I mind."

"Yeah, but I'm behind the bar in this get up" She spun around slowly, giving me a look at every edible inch of her small but curvaceous body. "I don't know—I could maybe dance on a one-on-one basis for certain individuals."

I sighed. "I understand, but I think you would be a natural."

"Maybe one day," she said.

I took great pleasure as I watched her ravishingly tempting ass and legs glide out of my office. I leaned back in my comfortable swivel chair. Life was good.

Then I heard Sugar's theme song blasting and the crowd's frenzied applause. I guzzled down my Hen and Coke and went downstairs to enjoy the show. I glanced at my watch. Sugar was on very early tonight.

Sugar wore a blue lacey number with an aqua color blue mask, the type with the feathers flaring out. Her skin glimmered with her patented sugar crystals reflecting the stage lights as she twisted this way and that. I admired the subtle placement of the two sugar cubes she wore, wanted to take them off of her perky nipples with my teeth. I'd be willing to wager I wasn't the only one with that thought on my mind.

I was standing in the VIP section, had the perfect overhead view of Sugar. I studied her movements, her body. She still appeared to own a certain familiarity to me. Something in my brain just clicked in that moment. It couldn't be! Tattoo, wig, mask or not, I knew I had seen this sexual predator before.

I hurried down the stairs that led to the VIP area and our offices, bypassed a series of patrons and security to get to one of the front rows that faced the main stage. It sat kind of like a boxing ring, surrounded on three sides by rows of drooling customers. Sugar noticed my descent her way, thought I saw her smirk. She grabbed the microphone and introduced one of her Georgian fellow dancers named Peaches.

Peaches came to the stage with that Florida bounce music playing. She was a pretty dark -skinned beauty with so much ghetto ass it didn't even look real, looked like a fake prosthesis placed over her ass. But them bouncing ass cheeks revealed to everyone present that that donkey was all flesh, was all ass. All you heard was whooping and shouting when Peaches executed a split, then a head stand, making those butt cheeks dance and jiggle.

I tried to get a glimpse of Sugar, but she went to the dressing rooms that were connected to the stage by a short hallway. I knew she had slipped away during the dancer exchange. Sugar had insisted a door leading outside be placed in her private dressing room, so she could come and go without being harassed was her logic. Now, though, I wasn't so sure. She had basically just given me the slip. Seemed to me she made it clear she didn't want me too close to her tonight.

I wonder...

Sampson   11

It was well after 2 a.m. when I walked through the exit at Sugarland. I had gotten a lap dance form that beach-ball-butt-having stripper named Peaches. Damn, what an ass! Peaches...they should call her ass teases, cause she wouldn't let me touch her Georgia peach, said something about being engaged and shit. Whatever!

I stumbled to my car parked in my spot just outside the front of the club, still feeling the effects of five Alabama-Slammas. I guess I didn't know when to say when. As I approached my vehicle, I laid red-rimmed eyes on a pretty little female leaning against my driver's side door. She was petite in stature but commanded a nice perky set of tits, coupled with a perfectly shaped ass, wasn't a donkey but it was a nice handful. She looked to be Latina, maybe from South America or some shit like that. I stared at her a moment, trying to discern the weird look she gave me as I approached, couldn't decide what her intent was by her puzzling expression, made me feel a little uneasy, though.

"Sorry to bother you, Papi," she said with a hint of Latin flavor. "But me have little car problem." She pointed toward the dark side road that was adjacent to the club. Kevin and Devin, my personal security picks, were obviously inside due to the club closing in about an hour. So the Latin vixen and I were the only two present in the parking area at the time.

I paused, contemplated going back in and letting one of my behemoths take care of her. She must have noticed my trepidation because she took a quick step toward me, got all in my personal space and spoke again more huskily. "I be very grateful, Papi…very grateful."

That did it!

"Sure, Mamacita," I slurred. "Guess I'm you're white…er…black knight tonight."

I allowed this pretty little thing to lead me past a dozen or so cars till we ended up near the end of the side street, a dead end, I might add.

She grabbed my crotch then. "Bueno." I think that was what she said.

Then as I started to cop a nice feel and explore her tantalizing mouth, she shrieked like I was committing bloody murder.

She screamed, "Now!"

Four hooded men in black emerged from a dark van I had failed to notice before. They all wore black gloves and ski masks, and were armed with small dark baseball bats. Shit! This was going to end badly for me.

The senorita placed her not-so-delicate knee right into

my groin. I remember going down to one knee. They all attacked as one. I was pummeled violently with everything they had. The beating lasted just a few seconds, but that was more than enough time to get their point across.

"Black sends his love, bitch," the senorita, now a hazy shadow spat. I heard laughter, heard them get back into their vehicle and speed off, their spinning tires kicking dirt and rocks in my face as they did so.

I rolled onto my back, vomited on myself, started to flex fingers, hands, arms, and legs to ascertain my injuries. Whew, nothing was broken, but I knew my face was more than likely fucked the hell up.

I slowly got to my feet, made it back to my car, and managed to drive home without anyone at the club being aware of my predicament. I didn't want a scene there, didn't want Black to see me weak. The short drive home was rough going. On the way, I was like, this was Deke's damn idea but my butt is taking the ass whipping for it.

I phoned Watts, got her voicemail from the jump. Damn! She was probably mad at my ass for standing her up tonight.

I finally made it home, noticed a light on that shouldn't have been. Fuck this! I got my Glock from my glove box, entered my house prepared to shoot first and take names later.

My house was pitch-black except for a flickering light coming from my master bedroom. I took the light to be candle in origin due to its flickering nature. It gave the atmosphere of my home an eerie feeling, made the hair stand up on the back of my neck.

The floor plan of my house was such that my bedroom was all the way in the back, past my kitchen, my living room, and a bathroom. There was a low moan emanating from my bedroom coupled with some low volume soft music.

I raised my gun, opened the door slowly. What I saw made me freeze in my tracks. Now I knew why Watts hadn't answered my call. She was engaged in a sweet 69 with a masked woman with a certain tattoo on her inner thigh. Sugar!

I just stared, my aches and pains all but forgotten. I had witnessed a similar scene to this before, only this was my home, in my bedroom and this was Sugar! I lowered my gun and entered the bedroom. The women didn't even bother to stop pleasing one another, couldn't and didn't take offense to that. I inhaled their scent as I began to slowly take my clothes off. With difficulty, I completed that task and walked to my master bathroom. Once inside, I turned on the shower, stepped in, and winced as the hot water hit my skin. I braved it, though, wanted to wash away the blood, vomit, and dirt that was caked all over my person. It would have been a very different shower indeed, had there not have been two—yes, two beautiful women sexing each other in my bed.

I had left the lights off, heard the door to the bathroom open, then Watts joined me in the shower, she kissed my bruises, washed me off very gently. When she got to Mr. Happy, she took him into soft hands and stroked him slow as she lathered the rest of my body with soap. I didn't really know it until that very moment, but I realized I loved

Watts. She held no judgment for me. It was that fact alone that opened my stupidly blind eyes to her then. She was what I needed in a partner.

"Watts—"

"Shhhhh…Samp…don't talk…just enjoy."

We stepped out of the shower. Sugar greeted us with towels, still with the mask on. She wore a simple black mask tonight, no feathers. There were no words spoken between us. We communicated with our eyes and bodies.

They led me to my bed, pushed me on my back, kissed each other, then came to me with pleasure on their minds, at least that was my belief.

As I lay back still feeling some residual effects of the beating I took, I couldn't help but grin. Funny how my misfortune of tonight turned out to be very fortunate. I had missed my date with Watts only to have her bring me what I had desired the most for the past few weeks. This was going to be some ending of the night, I thought. Surprisingly, didn't know it would turn out to be the night of my life!

Two sets of lips kissed me. Two tongues licked and savored my flesh, snaked around my snake. Two sets of hands roamed my body, made me grow, stroked my sex, and cupped my balls. I was sinfully in heaven! I moaned, exhaled deeply, had my head back eyeballing my ceiling, forgot all about my wounds. I gave into the pleasure, to the dirty deeds being performed on me.

Only sexual sounds were spoken then, the sounds of heat, sounds of passion.

Watts worked my shaft while Sugar made good use of

her tongue and mouth as she worked my sac over, giving each ball her undivided attention. She put them in her mouth, one then two, juggled them like jawbreakers.

"Oh—God!" I yelled as they continued to work me over.

They had me, former Officer Fucking Sampson, had me screaming like a little bitch. Frankly, I was! I was their bitch, their prisoner of lust, wished this could last forever…

I could feel my sex swelling, my head got bigger, sac got tighter. I was on the verge, was ready to erupt. I wasn't going to cum.

No!

I was going to explode, to fucking gush everywhere. I could feel it! To their credit, my sexual liberators never slowed. Must have sensed my impending climax was rapidly approaching, prompted them to suck harder, stroke faster, squeeze tighter.

"That's it! Yesss! That's fucking it!" I got light-headed. "Aaaaargh!" I blew my top with volumes of liquid bliss flying everywhere. It was so unbelievably good.

I never felt the poke. It was too subtle, too well timed and planned.

I should have fucking felt it, but didn't. Something was wrong, was irregular, this wasn't the aftermath or glow of an explosive orgasm. This was something else entirely.

I was drowning, falling, flying, headed toward the light. I tried to speak. My voice sounded garbled, like I was talking underwater. Somehow my speech was badly slurred.

Then I saw the face with the mask just mere inches

from my face. She grinned with the face of the devil. I couldn't move, felt like my body was submerged in quicksand.

"Enjoy it, Sample," she whispered. "Enjoy it, you sick fuck!"

"Noooo…d-d-did…Black…p-put…you up to this," I managed to convey.

"Black…hell no, baby." She held the syringe up to my face. "Nah, baby, this is compliments of good ole Sugar." She laughed. Her laughter sounded harsh, could feel the disdain in her tone.

Watts appeared. I wanted to scream at her to help me! She grabbed Sugar. I thought my salvation had arrived to help. Instead, Watts embraced Sugar, kissed her passionately. They turned to watch me fall further and further toward the void. Was so much I wanted to say, to share with Watts, but as I continued to slip away, the vision of her and Sugar's wicked grins locked on their visages, derailed me.

I was descending rapidly now. Falling! Wasn't moving physically. What was happening to me? What had they done?

I continued to fall.

Wasn't ascending…

There were no loved ones waiting for me, no deceased spouse, grandmother or parent.

No one of that consequence. Who I saw was a chunky cute teenager that I had forced myself on, saw Bones' scary ass then. He grinned at me, arms open as if to embrace me. I saw countless others I had wronged.

"Oh shit! No! No!" I screamed with all my might. Didn't know if I was heard by anyone, but I knew it mattered little if I had.

Jonesy appeared. I knew it was over then, knew what this all meant and where I was headed. He seemed to have grown in stature, had grown some new body parts as well. His head was deformed, had suddenly sprouted horns, teeth grew into fangs. He laughed, if you could call it that, more like a low growl.

"Welcome home," he said menacingly.

Funny, my last thought was, damn, that was the best skull I ever had!

Damn!

Then all went black.

Malcolm   12

I stayed till closing at Sugarland. I decided to help with the lockup procedures then head home. I texted my wife, which wasn't unusual when I was out late, but she never responded. I hoped nothing was wrong. Rochelle was a night owl much like myself, one huge thing, among others, that we had in common. I phoned her and got her voicemail immediately. Damn, Ro, what's up?

Then just as I got onto 70 southbound, I received a strange text from Sample. "Malcolm, need you to come over with the money. You know what we talked about earlier in the day. It has to be tonight." Huh, what the hell was Samp talking about? I phoned him, got his voicemail, so I sent a response to his text.

Sampson didn't live too far from me so I decided to go by his house. He was a little tipsy when he left the club. I asked if he wanted me to get one of the security guys to drive him home. He had declined, but still, I knew he wasn't quite himself. Probably just got me mixed up with someone else, but I still wanted to go and check on him.

It was at that moment I started to think about his meeting with Black earlier in the day. Sample had told me Black wanted 40 damn percent of our weekly take from club Sugarland. I wondered if he could be in some type of trouble. I put the pedal to the metal and sped the whole way to Sample's house. Unfortunately, I got a speeding ticket from my decision to make haste. Happened right before my Duke Street exit. Damn!

I finally made it to Sampson's house, pulled into his driveway behind his car. The house wasn't completely dark. It looked like there were some lights on in a few different rooms. I figured he must still be up and about. It was almost 4 in the morning.

I rang the doorbell, phoned his cell again. No answer to each. I knocked vigorously on the door, then just decided to try the damn knob. It turned, so I walked in.

Sampson's place was nice and neat. He was just that type of guy, always had been a neat freak. I smiled as I passed his living room with all his trophies and our multitude of team photos prominently displayed in a showcase.

I made my way all the way back to his bedroom, expecting to find his drunk ass passed out on the bed.

He was on the bed alright!

Sampson lay face down on his overly large bed. He was naked. The room smelled of sex, if you ask me, some funky sex would be my guess. "Damn, open a window or something, bro," I said.

I walked around the bed to see if I could wake him. It was then I noticed his eyes. They were wide open, staring at nothing in particular, was no light, no life that I could detect in them. I would never forget that look as long as I lived.

"Sampson! Sampson!" I screamed. I cradled his head in my lap as I checked his vitals. He was still warm, which meant he hadn't been deceased for very long. Tears streamed down my cheeks as I remembered all the good times me, Samp, and Deke had shared: college, basketball, bitches, even a business. We had shared a childhood, teenage years, and adulthood together.

I rocked him slowly before I came back to my senses and dialed 911. I gave them all the information that I had, still kind of in a foggy haze. I covered up my friend's body and walked out of the house to sit on the front steps. When I did, there were no fewer than 20 guns aimed at my body.

"Put your goddamn hands up now!" one of the police officers yelled.

"Huh—I called you...I just...I just found my friend lying dead on his bed," I said.

"One more time, Mister! Put your hands up and drop to your knees or so help me, you are a dead man!"

I complied, with confusion clearly etched on my face. They handcuffed and placed me into custody, was roughly thrown in the back of a patrol car. I didn't know why I was being treated so harshly. This can't be protocol, I reasoned. The more time I spent in that detained state, the more I started to wonder just what in the hell had happened to Sampson, how did they arrive here so fast, more importantly, why was I being held.

The police had no words for me other than the Miranda rights, never informed me of a thing, just took me on that ride that more than a few unfortunate black males have had the privilege of taking. A ride I had sworn I would never take, had lived my life to assure it would never happen.

But now, I was going downtown in the back of a police car!

Deke   13

I awakened to the image of a goddess. She still slumbered in my bed. I slowly pulled the covers off her naked body and admired the view, just watched the rise and fall of her chest as she slept. Rochelle had showed up shortly after I arrived home yesterday.

It had been her in the black SUV that had almost given me a heart attack, cruising past my house. She had borrowed one of her girlfriend's ride so she wouldn't be seen with her car at my place. Smart thinking, I guess.

Rochelle had come to me, expressed her frustrations with Malcolm and her need for something different, had practically forced herself onto me. I convinced myself I had no choice but to oblige her desires.

I was torn, though. Even though Rochelle belonged to me first, I had no right to her now. She had taken vows, had voiced her love before God and her family and friends that she would stand beside another man, a man who just happened to be like a brother to me.

I was really torn.

Once me and Rochelle got started, we couldn't stop. She had put it on me something fierce last night. I had slept for a few uninterrupted hours after my third orgasm. To tell the truth, I really don't recall drifting off, but I sure remember the love making.

I put the covers back over her, walked to the kitchen, turned on my television to the morning news, and walked to the driveway hoping the paperboy's aim was decent today.

I noticed right away Rochelle's truck was parked in a different spot on the street than it had been last night. I had a short driveway, and my two vehicles occupied my only two spots, therefore Rochelle had to park on the street. But she had parked just ahead of my driveway last night, almost in front of my neighbor's house, but now the truck was behind my driveway, while my neighbor's car was where her truck had been.

No big deal, I guess, just meant she must have gone out while I was comatose from all that great sex.

I walked back into my house, and that's when I heard the scream.

'What—"

Rochelle was in the kitchen. A carton of eggs were at her feet. I followed her gaze to the television.

"Once again, Officer Rodney Sampson was found dead early this morning in his home in Durham County. Police believe he was a victim of foul play. Malcolm Jason Lee was taken into police custody at the crime scene. Officer

Sampson was suspended earlier in the month following an investigation into the murder of his late partner Officer Steven Jones. We will have more on this breaking news." The reporter continued to inform the public on the next subject of a new restaurant opening in Raleigh, North Carolina.

I was flabbergasted, stood there dumbfounded.

Rochelle screamed, "Oh—no! Malcolm! I've got to get to Malcolm! He must have been trying to reach me. I have to go to my husband, Deke."

I was still stunned. "Huh…ah…s-sure, Ro." I still couldn't believe it, couldn't process what the reporter had just said. The two most important people in my life, one dead, the other in police custody, I presumed because they thought he did it.

"No! Nooooo!" It was all I could manage. Rochelle came to me, hugged me tight. She took charge then, led me to my couch, talked to me in soothing tones.

"I have to go, Deke," she whispered.

"So do I," I said

"Give me some time to gather the details then I'll call you, OK, Deke?"

"What…no, Rochelle. I have to go to Durham, have to see Samp's family if nothing else."

She nodded her understanding, got dressed quickly then and peeled rubber leaving my dwelling as fast as she could.

I phoned Sampson's sister, Bree. She told me what she knew, which wasn't much, and I told her that I was on the way to her parents' home.

The drive to Durham from Raleigh was so surreal. I

was in a mental fog, didn't understand what was going on but one person kept popping into my thoughts. One person's face kept clouding my vision. I had to find out the truth, cause if it was who I suspected, I would find a way to kill the sonofabitch!

I'm coming, Black! Crazy or not!

I'm fucking coming!

You mess with one, you mess with us all!

Malcolm 14

Once the police got me downtown, booked me, and left me in a cell for hours, I was finally able to find out a little bit of information regarding Sample. Apparently he was murdered, given a lethal dose of heroin, a dose the police believed I gave him; based on an anonymous tip.

They took me to a room and started bombarding me with all sorts of questions, some that were very strange to me. I was no damn fool, though, and refused to answer or say anything until I could speak with my attorney. I knew whatever one said to the authorities without a lawyer present could be twisted to whatever angle they wanted. So I just sat quietly while they tried unsuccessfully to get me to answer their questions. I sat and soaked up the knowledge that my friend was dead, that I was the prime suspect and that my wife was nowhere to be found.

I was just glad that my twin boys were at their grandparents' house near Greensboro for the week. I hadn't had the chance to contact anyone except my lawyer Patrick Fitz.

Fitz was not only my attorney but a good friend. We attended the same schools growing up, and Patrick was well respected in the triangle area. He had a great win percentage as well, which was what I was counting on, but I knew I had nothing to do with Sample's death. Still, that didn't mean anything unless I could prove it. When I worked and lived in D.C., I had several friends and acquaintances whose profession dealt with or in the law. I knew the police must have some strong evidence against me to treat me the way they had.

Footsteps were falling my way. Patrick Fitz walked the long narrow hallway to my cell.

I was taken to another private room to confer with him. The look he gave me instantly almost made my heart stop.

"Pat, what's going on? Why did they arrest me? I called 911 for Christ sakes, right after I found Sample's body "

Patrick Fitz looked me calmly in the eye. He said, "Malcolm, let's cut to the chase."

"OK."

"It doesn't look good. You didn't do this, right?"

"Do this—no Patrick! Hell no, I didn't kill Sampson. He was like my fucking brother. Shit, what the fuck is going on here?"

"OK, Mal, first tell me what happened tonight and leave nothing out."

I told Fitz everything I had done that day, tried to recall every minute detail so as not to miss anything. I did leave out the fact that I had followed my wife to the jailhouse where I witnessed the somewhat-heated exchange between her and Sample, just didn't think that it was pertinent to my situation now. I told Fitz about the strange text messages I had received from Sampson after I left the club, how they prompted me to drop by his house in the wee hours of the morning in the first place. I recalled the state his house was in, how I found him, and how I checked his vitals and dialed the police.

"Is that absolutely everything, Mal?" Fitz asked, his tone somewhat accusatory.

"The way I remember it," I said.

"OK, now let me ask you some questions. Some of these may be difficult to answer, but I need you to be extremely candid and brutally honest with me."

I nodded.

"Do you use drugs, Malcolm?"

"Hell no, I barely drink alcohol. You know that, Pat."

"OK. You said before that you and Officer Sampson were like brothers."

"Yes...me...Samp and Deke. You remember they use to call us the Triplets on the basketball court."

"Yeah, I remember. Well...uh...Mal, did you and Sampson have a relationship of a different nature than the one you are describing to me now?"

I stood then, didn't like what Fitz was trying to imply.

"What do you mean, Pat?"

Fitz took a deep breath, relaxed his shoulders. "Were you lovers, Malcolm?" He said this with such reluctance, it came out as a faint whisper.

A whisper that I heard as if he shouted the question. I

yelled," Hell No!" I was stunned by the question, it came out of left field to me. "Look, I'm no homophobe by any stretch of the imagination. I have gay friends, have contributed to gay rights causes and such, but, Fitz, I'm all about the cat."

"OK, Mal. I had to ask."

"And as far as I know, Sample didn't flow that way either."

"Why the hell would you ask something like that?"

Fitz said, "First let me say, you need to let them take your blood. If what you're telling me is true, it could definitely benefit you right now."

"My blood," I queried.

"Yes, Malcolm, they need your blood for two reasons. One, to drug test you."

"I'm clean, Pat. Bring the test on."

"Number…uh…two… reason is, they need a sample of your DNA."

"Huh? DNA sample?"

"Well yes, Malcolm. Sampson had semen in his rectal area, and well they need to know if it's yours." Fitz started sweating profusely then, looked uncomfortable revealing this to me, not as uncomfortable as I felt hearing this bullshit, though.

My mind starting working in overdrive, felt the blood rush to my face in anger. Fitz observed me very closely. "Get them in here as soon as fucking possible to test me, Pat," I confidently stated.

"Good, Mal. That could go a long way into clearing you."

"Wait, Pat…'go a long way'… Why wouldn't it prove my innocence if the DNA doesn't match?"

"Well, we still have more circumstantial evidence to deal with."

"What freaking evidence, Fitz? What?"

"OK, well, let's take the text messages, Malcolm."

"What was Sampson referring to when he asked you to bring the money?"

"That's just it. I don't know. I just figured he sent me a text meant for someone else."

"Uh-huh," Fitz didn't look convinced by my answer." What about the last text Mal. The one where he says, I quote 'We need to tell Rochelle now' end quote."

"I never got a text saying that."

"According to your phone records, you did, at about 3:30 a.m."

I was speechless, just dumbfounded. Then something surfaced in my thoughts. "Pat, I called Sampson when I got to his house because he didn't answer the doorbell. That was around 3:30, so how could he have texted me if he were dead?"

"I will make a note to check the times, Malcolm."

"What are they thinking, Fitz? Why am I in the police's crosshairs?"

"Well, Detective Davis's theory goes as follows. You and Officer Sampson were lovers on the DL. Sampson started to blackmail you for money. You came over and had one more fling before killing him to keep him from outing you to your wife."

"That is fucking ridiculous, Patrick. First off, Sample,

myself, and Deke are business partners. We own club Sugarland. I don't know if you've seen it, but the place stays packed. Sample didn't need to blackmail me for cash. Second and most importantly, I am not a fucking gay man!"

"OK, Malcolm, I believe you. I'm just making you aware of their evidence and their theory. Also, according to an off-duty officer working security at a strip club called...ah...Black's, you were seen having an altercation with Officer Sampson where witnesses reported that your wife was mentioned by Sampson and that set you off."

"Yes, but..."

"So that's true, Malcolm. Sampson's phone records indicate that he sent texts to your wife earlier in the night using some well...colorful language. Also, your prints were found on the syringe that he was injected with."

"This is crazy. I've never handled a syringe. I hate needles. This is a fucking setup, Pat, pure and simple."

"Yes, well that's what they have. So you can clearly see, every spec of evidence, all points its finger at you, Mal."

I put my head in my hands, wanted to vomit. I felt sick. I couldn't imagine that all this was happening to me. My friend was dead, had been snuffed out, murdered. To tell the truth, if I didn't know I wasn't guilty, I would believe I did it due to the mountain of evidence. I concluded that my only salvation would come from the DNA testing.

"I didn't do this, Fitz. I don't give a shit what they have. I didn't kill Sample or have any kind of sex with him whatsoever." I was pleading with him now. "You gotta get me out of here, Pat."

"I'm doing my best, Mal. Sampson might have been on suspension, but he was still a cop, and they don't take cop killers lightly."

I just stared at Fitz when he said killer. His cell rang then. "Fitz...yes, he's holding up as well as can be. I'm almost done here. OK. I'll tell him. That was Rochelle... Malcolm, she's here, waiting to see you."

"Rochelle," I said.

"Yes, look I'm going to get to work to try and get bail appointed. Hopefully the judge will not see you as a flight risk and just give you a high-figure bail, which I'm sure you can handle. Correct?"

"Yeah, Fitz, just get me bail. I don't care how much it is. I want out of this hell hole."

"OK, Mal, give me a few hours. In the meantime, talk to your wife. She didn't sound too good."

"Fitz...,"

"Yeah...,"

"Thanks, man."

Hey, this is what you pay me for. Handsomely, I might add. Hang in there, bro." He walked away. I just sat there, nervous, afraid, and unsure.

I heard her heels clicking on the tiled floor. I looked up. Rochelle had arrived, and she did not look like the supportive spouse.

She was pissed!

Sugar 15

One down...

I glared at myself in the mirror sitting at my vanity. I was me now, the regular me, Sugar had fled my flesh for a while, left me to my own devices. I had just finished removing the very real looking fake-tattoo I had learned to apply. I was glad I had fucked that art major last year. I smiled. He taught me a great many things removable paints. He learned somethings from me as well. That was in the past. It was time for the present now.

I studied my face then, the face she covered with masks. She did so to protect my identity, wasn't due to her being ashamed of anything. I could see why some considered me attractive, why they eyed my curves, my full breasts, ample ass, and purely African lips. Don't get me wrong, I wasn't admiring myself. I was just taking in the physical characteristics that Sugar used to her advantage. She found ways to highlight my flawless light mocha-colored skin tone, my long eyelashes, sexy smile, and very generous curves. It was true, I was a pretty woman, but Sugar took that pretty, made it sexual, made it seductive, transformed pretty to desirable. Sugar took who I was and improved it tenfold.

Once the mask was on, Sugar was on, would shine like I didn't. Sugar didn't even use my voice, developed her own, was different in a sultry kind of way. Sugar was her own entity within me, built on rage, born for a singular purpose.

Revenge!

At first, she was my instrument, my creation. Now, she controlled herself, made up her own rules. Vengeance was her initial fuel. It gave her the sustenance to remain focused on her objective. Yet Sugar had tasted flesh, loved the power sex had over the weak. She grew increasingly drunk with it, was on the verge of becoming addicted to the other desires. I just had to trust she would complete our tasks before she succumbed to the various temptations.

We had planned for this, really never knew we would get the chance but fate had intervened on our behalf. Now all these fucks would fall. They would fall and die. I smiled. My reflection mimicked the act. Yes, she was rubbing off on me a little bit at a time.

I must admit, I admired Sugar. I envied her sexual freedom, her lack of inhibitions. Sugar could command man and woman alike with her sexuality. They routinely fell to their knees to do her bidding. Sugar was like a goddess, a deity whom they worshipped because they wanted to fuck her. Yes, that was it! It was all about the fucking really. That was where her true power lay. She was one of those women who embraced that power. She was Lilith, Adam's first wife, born of her own flame. She was uncontrollable, temptation incarnate, thrived in the throes of her desires, was too much for Adam to handle, made from her own mold, not taken from Adam's rib. Lilith/Sugar was individual, could stand alone. Eve benefitted from following her, from coming second. Eve learned her lessons well from the first.

My sex existed as Eve, subservient, obedient, and welcoming to the Adams. While my mind was ruled by Lilith...the temptress, the sexual predator, the dominate gender. All... men and women alike would bow to my will for a chance to dwell in my Garden of Eden.

I stared at the masks then. They were lined up on my vanity table. Each mask seemed to represent a different emotion. I picked one up, brought it up to the light, stared.

Masks...

I had always been fascinated by the comic book character that used Bats and Masks to evoke fear, not the child's cartoon version, but rather the true character, "The Dark Knight." It was interesting to me how a simple object like a mask could transform one's personality. Millionaire playboy Mr. Wayne, became a violent vigilante on a quest for revenge by simply donning a mask.

I, like him, had a quest of my own. Sugar was my alter ego. We weren't heroes, though. We were women with a promise to keep, a promise made in the presence of blood, a blood pact that was sealed years ago. I looked at the mask again, saw it for what it was, its color was red. Then, I secured it to my face. Sugar instantly came forth.

$ $ $

I chose a nice purple lacey number for tonight's performance. The little kitty I had to manipulate tonight loved me in purple. She kept me in purple thongs and lingerie, and I kept her wet and gushing. I grinned, just thinking about how she was putty in my hands and how this bitch thought she loved me so. It was time to move more pieces in my game of chess.

I dialed her number, got wet myself with the anticipation.

"Hello."

"Watts, baby, we need to meet," I purred.

"So soon? I thought we agreed to lie low for awhile, so as not to be seen together."

"Yeah, we won't be. Meet me at room 237at the Holiday Inn Express on New Bern Avenue in Raleigh at around midnight," I said.

"OK, baby, can't wait to see you," she sounded so clingy, just needed her to stay that way a little while longer.

"Can't wait to taste you, baby," I said. "I'll bring the caramel if you bring the vanilla."

"Is this business or pleasure, Shug?"

"It's always both when it comes to us, baby. See you there."

"OK, midnight then."

That being done, I had to make a stop at the Bio-Tech

Research Center in RTP before I left for work.

I finished dressing, put on some bright red lipstick, then gloss for the effect I was looking for, gave them a real nice sheen of color. The fool I had to meet always commented on them and shit, like he could sweet talk my panties off. Please! He wouldn't take long to tame, though. In fact, if he secured what I asked for, he just might get a little bonus in the parking lot. I gave myself a once over again, then smiled.

Sugar was on the prowl!

Malcolm   16

I hadn't been able to get an ounce of sleep the few hours I had been incarcerated, almost stood the whole time in my quaint six-by-nine room, courtesy of the Durham Police Department.

When finally I had to sit, I laid back on the hard-as-steel bunk and let my mind drift. Wanted to see if I could come up with whoever wanted Sampson dead and who would frame me for it. My conclusions were not agreeable to my sanity. They kept leading me back to one person. My wife! Rochelle…'til death do we part.'

After Fitz departed, Rochelle entered the visiting area, I had to be escorted to. All eyes went to her immediately, which was typical for her, but she didn't wear the typical look she reserved for me and only me, her goddamn husband!

She sat, gave me eyes of disdain at first, eyes of scrutiny. My heart sank. Rochelle, the love of my life, my soul mate, did something unexpected. When I think about it now, it still makes my blood boil. She leaned closer to the Plexiglas barrier, held my gaze, like a cobra holds the gaze of a rat. Then quite simply, she smiled, smiled the smile of the elated.

She looked me over. "Hello, Malcolm, just what the hell have you gotten yourself into?" Her statement sounded hollow to me, like she was feigning concern.

"Rochelle, where have you been? I have tried reaching you and so has Fitz. I—"

"I was busy," she tsked. "Looks like you've gone and done something even I can't help you with, Mal."

I couldn't understand. Why was she being so cavalier about all this shit. "Rochelle, this is serious," I said. "They believe I killed Sampson and what's more, they think we were fucking lovers."

"I heard, Mal. It's all over the morning news. Do you have any idea how you made me look in front of my parents? Do you know the scorn you've placed on your boys with this damn scandal? I told you, your low-ass-class friends would bring you down eventually, didn't I, Malcolm?"

"Rochelle, are you serious…scandal? They are charging my ass with goddamn murder!" I put my head in my hands. "I can't believe this. Here I thought you were my rock, my backbone, and you sitting here like this shit is no big deal."

"What do you want me to do, Malcolm, huh? Damage control? She sighed. "I'm here, aren't I? I just can't believe you." She closed her eyes, then opened them. "OK, Mal, what do you need me to do?"

"I need you to be my damn wife for one, to have my back. You know me better than anyone, Ro. You know that I didn't...that I couldn't... do this." I was on the verge of tears by then. "Rochelle, I need your love now more than ever."

"You need my love, Malcolm," she said sarcastically. Ain't this a bitch. You been running around on my ass for years, even got me in some of your freaky-ass shit, taken our marriage vows for granted and now, when you got your dick in a sling, you need my love." She smiled thinly. "You've always had it. That's what's so pathetic. It takes something like this to make you realize who is most important."

"Rochelle, I—,"

"Don't worry, Mal, I won't abandon you, not now. I'm just upset and venting. Yes, you're right. I know you could never have done what they say. What has Patrick had to say? Can you bond out?"

"Well, the magistrate denied me bail when they first brought me in, but I will have a bail hearing in a couple of hours, so maybe then. It will probably be a large sum. We might have to liquidate some assets."

"I'll take care of that," she assured me, was almost too eager, though. "I just need a figure to work with."

I exhaled, finally saw a glimmer of hope, was glad my wife was here and standing by me. She just seemed to be acting a little strange, like she was a bad actress in one of those B movies.

"Have you called your company, Malcolm? I'm sure

someone at your office has heard the news by now."

"It's taken care of," I answered. "What I'm really waiting on is this DNA test to come back. It could exonerate me instantly."

"Is that right?" she queried.

"Yes, Rochelle. It will definitely prove it's not my semen they found at the scene."

"Ewwww, "she teased.

"Rochelle, please be serious. Someone did kill Sample, though, and that person is still out there."

Fitz appeared then. He walked up to Rochelle, gave her a hug, and whispered something in her ear, which immediately changed her facial expression to that of surprise.

"OK, I'll go get some coffee or something" She moved swiftly. "I'll be right back, baby." Now Rochelle sounded too sweet, almost too damn loving. She never left to get the coffee though.

I glared at Fitz. He reciprocated my stare, then he inhaled deeply. "Malcolm," he said. "We have a serious problem."

"What is it now, Patrick? What else could there be?"

"Do you remember giving blood to your company in 2006 while you were living in Washington, DC?"

"Uh…yes…we had a huge government contract then and every employee had to have a DNA profile due to the top-secret nature of the project. So what has that got to do with my situation now?"

"Well, you were logged into a national database then, most police departments are connected to all those databases and…well…"

"Well what, Fitz?"

"The computer came back with a positive match, Malcolm. It's your semen. I'm sorry."

I couldn't have heard him right, but he had indeed said what he had said. I just sat there stunned, unable to respond. Rochelle had been standing behind Fitz as he relayed the news to me. She didn't notice that I had noticed. She cracked a smile. I saw that expression as clear as day, as she overheard. My mind existed in a cloudy haze after Fitz laid the bombshell and I witnessed Rochelle's demeanor.

After returning to my cell, I lay in my bunk playing back the latest events in my mind. I couldn't help but wonder. Did Rochelle have anything to do with me being framed and arrested for Samp's murder?

One thing I did know for certain now, I was fucked!

Deke 17

It had been two days since Sampson's death. I still couldn't believe he was gone, and what's more, Malcolm was rotting in jail for his murder. I don't care what evidence the Po-po's claimed to have. I knew both my bros, this just had to be a serious screw job.

I had gone to see Malcolm the first day of his arrest. He was in bad shape but hopeful. He was catching it two fold, though, hurting over the death of a friend, but also scared of losing his life to prison over something he didn't do. I tried to reassure him that no one would believe these false allegations, but hard evidence is hard evidence. Malcolm was no fool. I had to admit, I questioned whether or not he could have done it for a brief moment, but once I visited with him, I knew he was innocent.

I knew it was hard on his twin boys now, since Mal was denied bail, he didn't want them to visit him in jail. We both prayed and held on to the belief that somehow Patrick

Fitz could work his magic and get him home. At least he had the best lawyer money can buy, and I knew Fitz would stop at nothing to get to the truth.

It was hard for me to look at Mal initially. I just knew he could see my betrayal, could smell Rochelle's scent seeping from my pores. It was all in my mind, though. Malcolm was just glad, was grateful even, just to see me. I felt like shit the whole while but knew I had to keep a positive front for him.

I assured him I would keep a watchful eye on his family and continue to run club Sugarland, because we needed a successful business more than ever now. Legal fees are not cheap.

I had my own theory about Sample's death, and today I was going to get some damn answers. I lay in my bed awake early in the morning with all these thoughts stirring in my mind. Movement to my left broke my contemplations. She leaned on her elbow facing me, gave me lustful eyes then snuggled up. Rochelle put her head on my chest, then lower, took her tongue, traced circles around the crown of my dick. She must have been a witch doctor in a past life, had mastered the art of bringing the dead back to the living. I didn't think it was possible for me to fly full staff once more, but alas, Rochelle had her sexual gifts. So, before I could start my day, to try and learn hidden truths, I had to fuck my best friend's wife once more with feeling. I was falling under her spell, didn't know what I could do but obey my own desires, my urges. Her thirst matched my own, could not be quenched once we had a taste of our carnal cravings.

She equally turned me off and on at the same time, was both ashamed and sexually satisfied with myself.

"Rochelle, I need to get up," I protested.

"Yeah, you need to get all up in this pussy." She opened her flower to me then. "This is yours now, Deke, want it or not?"

I fought with my desire, my lust, my conscience.

I lost that battle again.

$ $ $

What the fuck is wrong with me? I asked that of myself and not for the first time. Yes, it was true, I've always longed, even lusted after Rochelle, but this just wasn't right, felt so damn good, though.

I would have to make some tough decisions soon.

I was headed toward downtown Durham, to the jailhouse. I was going to look in on Malcolm, but my purpose was with another.

Black...

The time had come for a face to face. I had to know the truth, had to know if he had my brotha killed.

As I walked into the visitors area, I noticed all eyes instantly fell in my direction. Durham was a small city in certain aspects. Word travels fast, especially in lockup. I was a bit nervous, but I refused to let it show, used my anger to mask my uncertainty.

Black stood as I approached, did that for my benefit. His hulking form was usually an intimidating image. Not today, not for me. I strolled to the seat in front of him as calm as I could muster. I must have been convincing. He appeared put off by my down-to-business demeanor.

"Have a seat, Black," I said.

"Oh, you giving me orders now, little cuz?" His voice was harsh, edgier than usual. Not the tone I was accustomed to.

"Naw, Black. Stand if you want. Do what you want, but I thought this was a meeting." Black nodded to the guard who escorted him in. That gesture made him fall a few steps back, gave us a modicum of privacy.

"So what you want, Deke? You come here to talk about my money or to make funeral arrangements?" He chuckled at his last uttered words.

I remained calm, knew what type of nigga I was dealing with. Black always tried to gain the upper hand right out the gate.

"What arrangement might I be trying to make with you, Black?"

"Yours, muthafucka, I hear you all alone at club Sugarland now. Maybe we can –uh, kiss and make up." He smiled evilly. "Become partners. I can let bygones be bygones if you can." Black spread his hands before him in a gesture of peace.

"You threatened my life, Black, threatened the life of Sample, as well." I got closer to the Plexiglas barrier. "You can cut the Black Godfather routine. Answer this, did you have Sample killed?"

He looked me dead in the eye. I studied his pockmarked face, the scars left by acne and razor bumps, studied the lines in his forehead, reminded me of a pit bull who fought often, fought and won. Funny that his nickname was Black 'cause the nigga was high-yella, which made his scars even more distinguished.

I waited for a response. His delay was anticipated, knew he would play mind games with me. I decided to push, make the hood surface from his cool demeanor.

"Answer me, muthafucka! Did you have Sample killed?"

"Deke, watch your temper, nigga," he said, still calm.

"I'll excuse it for now, 'cause I know your punk ass is grieving."

"Black—"

"But know this, little cuz, I didn't have Sample killed. Truth be told, I liked the dumb fuck." He sounded surprisingly sincere.

"No, Deke... it wasn't me. Besides, word on the street is he was butt-fucked then shot full of smack or vice versa. Anyway, not my style, and I gotta say that shit surprised even me, always thought Samp chased the cat."

"He did, Black. He did."

"But there is one thing I will say."

"Yeah..."

"If I was gonna have anybody offed, it would be you, nigga, unless you trying to come up with my 40 percent or partner up. Remember that, little cuz...'cause your days are numbered."

"So what, Black, you don't scare me. Maybe you got half of Durham on your cracked-out-ass payroll, but fuck that. You don't scare me."

"You got seven days to come to an understanding."

"Seven days?"

"Yeah, nigga, was gonna give you two but I'm feeling generous." He grinned wickedly.

"In a week, Ima be out of this hell hole…in a week, Deke."

My mind whirled then. I had one fucking week left, that I was sure of. I said, "It will be a short stint of freedom, nigga, if I find out you had Samp killed. That's my word!"

The tension in the visiting area was as thick as some Hogheaven's Brunswick stew. The faces that eyeballed me did so with shocked but approving expressions. They all knew that no one ever talked to Black the way I had, talked and lived that is. I was determined to buck that trend, though.

"You know Sample came in here not so long ago spouting that same kind of lip you using. Where is Mister Sampson now—oh yeah—he's dead. You can join him very easily, Deke," he stated calmly.

"Fuck you, Black. You must've forgotten who your damn bookkeeper was. Ain't they about to get you for conspiracy anyway?" It was my turn to smile.

"Do you, little cuz," he said with visible malice.

"I will."

He stood… I stood. I was possibly staring at my grim-reaper, but I knew he was staring at his death as well. I was through taking shit from anyone. Period!

"Seven days," He said, then turned and stalked out.

I got up and paced the hallway, waited for Malcolm to come down.

We had some things to discuss.

Malcolm 18

Two days had passed since my incarceration. It felt more like 20. I wasn't built for this shit. I had been placed in solitary due to a suicide watch. I had Fitz to thank for that, but that was only going to work for a short time.

I spent my time breaking down possible motives and suspects for my frame job. Still didn't know how my DNA wound up on Samp or how my fingerprints got on the syringe. My summations were so farfetched. They even left me with the conclusion of my guilt. There had to be something I was missing, some link that I had overlooked.

Black had word sent to me. Still had the piece of paper with the chicken scratch handwriting clutched in my hand. It read simply, "Forty-percent nigga" with a crude smiley face drawn on the other side. I knew it was Black just messing with me, but it still had me unnerved. I was in his world now and didn't like what that meant for me. I always felt like he tolerated me as I did him for Rochelle's benefit. But now, how long could Rochelle keep him at bay.

Rochelle. In the last two days I had only seen her that one time on the first day of this madness. I had spoken with her briefly on two occasions, but got the feeling all wasn't right in Happyville.

As I approached the visiting area to have a sit-down with Deke, I decided to ask him to do some snooping for me. I needed him to check on Rochelle's comings and goings.

Deke look flustered, like he was the one facing murder charges. I knew I looked like hammered shit, but he looked like his sanity was on the verge as well.

"Sit down, Deke," I said. "What's new in the land of the free?"

He sat down hard. "Black," he simply stated.

"What about him?" I asked.

"He's going to kill or have me killed, Malcolm, and I think he did Samp in as well."

As much as I wanted to have that psychopath blamed for this, I just didn't think it was his style. Oh, he would have been clever about it so no fingers pointed his way, but it would have been more gangsta, more cold blooded, than a gay drug overdose murder. It just didn't fit.

"Well, what's this about him going to kill you," I asked, seeing Deke was visibly shaken.

"We just had it out. He wants the 40 percent or to be full partner in the club. Told me I had a week to think on it."

"A week—that's not a whole lot of time, and is he

forgetting that I have a major stake in the club."

"Man, he don't give a shit. He figures since Samp is dead and you locked up, the time is now to get what he wants."

"I guess you're right. What are you going to do?"

"What should I do?"

"Deke, I honestly don't know, but think twice before you cross this fool. You know he's..."

"I'm fucking Rochelle, Malcolm," Deke stated matter-of-factly.

I must not have heard him right. I was in the middle of telling him to take precautions to secure his safety and . . ."What the hell did you just say," I asked, perplexed.

"I—uh—I'm so sorry, Mal." He looked me dead in the eye, did so like a man, like a man who was banging my wife. I could tell he struggled with the telling, with revealing to me his sins, their fucking sins. Then, just like that, he got up and walked away, never looked back.

I had no words, didn't have any more brain matter to calculate this new issue so I just stood, nodded to the guard and walked the mentally long corridor back to my cell.

What a fucking day.

Sugar   19

"**Oh, shit!**" He squealed like a little bitch. I raised my head from his lap, reached over and wiped my mouth with his standard butt-ugly Carolina blue tie. The look he gave me, one of shock or disbelief, made me laugh uncontrollably. Dr. Jacob Lawson was a middle age, married and respected member of the scientific community who worked in RTP, he was also my bitch. I secured his services one night after he secured a nice lap dance complete with fringe benefits from me. He had access to some vital merchandise I needed to execute my plans, and I knew just how to obtain it from the good doctor.

"Thanks, Jake," I said smiling. I watched him pull his boxers then his slacks up, knew he hadn't noticed the lipstick I left on both. Bet his wife would.

"What do you plan on doing with that stuff," he asked.

"Research, Jake. I told you that. Just need it to complete some experiments for my degree in bio-toxin sciences."

"Biology, huh…" He wasn't convinced. But that head he just got made him not give a shit. "I could get into a lot of trouble if they find that missing," he whined.

"Please, Jacob. They got hundreds of gallons of the stuff in there. Who in the hell is going to miss a beaker full." I palmed his crotch. "Don't worry. I know what I'm doing. It's our little secret, OK?."

He nodded. "Money," he ordered.

I gave over the bills and sealed the deal with tongue, let him taste his own produce.

I said, "You can put your ring back on now, Jake. It never mattered to me anyway."

"Ring," he asked dumbfounded.

"Yeah, your wedding ring, Jake…put it back on."

He looked nervous but complied.

"Now, that's better. We don't need to lie to one another about things of that sort." I started to get out of his car.

"One more thing, can I see you Saturday. Please say yes."

I did some quick calculations. "Sure, baby, you got a sweet tooth for old Sugar now."

He grinned. "I suppose so."

I winked at him then exited his car, planning on seeing him one last time if at all. It would be never if he's lucky and if he's not, well, Sugar would just have to keep that date.

I placed the vial he acquired for me in a small cooler packed with frozen cold packs then walked to my car. He watched my backside the entire time, stared as I slid into the driver's seat.

Men are so predictable that way.

I arrived at the Holiday Inn Express about an hour before Watts, had just enough time to set up, wanted her to feel comfortable, relaxed even. She was crucial to my plans, vital to finishing what I had started. She would never really know just how important her role truly was, at least not if all went accordingly.

I heard a faint knock just as I was finishing making Watts' current favorite drink, Dirty H2O.

"Hey, baby . . ."I didn't finish my statement cause Watts jumped me, pushed me onto the queen size bed, put her tongue in my mouth, went Cousteau as she went from tongue kissing me down, to sucking my breasts, to diving in my Bermuda. "Watts, damn... business... oh shit, first."

She raised moistened lips from between my thighs, sighed, and said, "Just wanted a little taste is all."

"Yeah, a little taste my ass, bitch." I grinned. "You t-trying to get my legs trembling up in this, mutha."

I sat up, maneuvered her to a sitting position. "This is important. The plan is coming together so we can't fuck up now."

"You a conniving bitch, Sugar, but we going to be on easy street if this shit works."

"All you got to do is keep servicing that bitch and feeding information like you've been doing, Watts. Then when the time is right, all of our jailbird's money will be coming our way before he knows what hit him."

She grinned in my face. "Pure fucking genius, Sugar. That's why I love your fine ass."

Was this bitch serious? Yeah, she loved me all right, loved them multiple orgasms I routinely gave her with this diamond studded tongue. But she had it all wrong, was naïve to my true machinations. Watts assumed my angle in all of this was monetary. She had no clue. It was even simpler than greed. Vengeance!

It burned in me, was my purpose for being. I eyed her curves then, reached over the overnight stand and produced her drink.

"Dirty Water, just like you like it, Watts. Now tell me, did you take care of the little job at the jailhouse I asked you to do?"

She tossed back her drink, finished with two gulps. "Of course, Shug. The money was transferred this morning."

"Excellent. Can we trust they will handle things without fucking the shit up?" I asked.

"Those two will take care of it swiftly. They've handled this sort of thing before, besides I told them they might get a bonus on top of the money. They both want me to join them in a threesome, you know."

I smiled, pleased that that part of the plan was done. Watts was such a whore. I appreciated her lack of sexual inhibitions though. It pained me a little that I couldn't witness what I was paying for. I would just have to gain satisfaction knowing it would be a total shock and surprise to the party involved; when the deed was completed. My plans were moving forward. I had to stay even more focused now. I gave Watts the other drink, watched her gulp that one down as well. Lovely…

I then pulled her back to where she wanted to be, her

head between my thighs, tongue making figure eights and circles in my na-na.

"Hmmm...I love the taste of Sugar," she said. She began to use her hands in conjunction with that talented tongue of hers.

I just decided to lie back, enjoy the moment. Like me, Watts loved to please, only our motivations were different. My motives were strictly business, while hers were primal, very different indeed. I didn't care about her reasons now, just wanted the release she was providing.

Shit, business was over. Was time for some pleasure.

Malcolm   20

Day three behind these ever closing-in walls had me feeling numb. I daydreamed while awake, had nightmares while I slept, couldn't think straight after the unexpected bomb Deke had dropped on me.

He and Rochelle.

Deke and my wife.

They were sinning together while I was shackled, chained, utterly powerless to do a damn thing about it. My heart was breaking with every breath I took. I had to finally realize the undeniable truth: Rochelle had never really loved me but had loved the life I had provided. She showed her true colors as soon as I was in dire straits.

It was true, I wasn't a murderer but I sure as hell wanted to strangle that bitch now. Yes, squeeze the fucking life out of the mother of my children, the woman I stood before God and proclaimed my undying love to.

She was my Delilah, my Kryptonite, and the knowledge

that she was sharing my best friend's bed was almost the last straw to take what little sanity I had left. But as I gazed at the small photo of my twins, I vowed to not let insanity win. Somehow, someway, I would find a way out of this mess, just had to hold on to some type of hope. No, not hope. Anger! I could use it to fuel me, could make my own mental plans of retribution. Yeah, that's what I'll do, plot some revenge of my own.

"Malcom Lee, you have a visitor on their way to see you." That was the guard buzzing my room.

It must be Fitz. I didn't think I would see him until later in the afternoon, he had told me he had court this morning. I got myself together, collected my thoughts, and strolled down the corridor to the visiting area ignoring the guard at my side.

Waiting for me there was pure evil, was demented in the way this entity tortured my soul. Rochelle stood and smiled. She was clothed in a tight-fitting red dress, ruby-red lipstick, and rosy red pumps. The top of her dress was cut low for effect, displaying her ample cleavage and drawing any spectator's eyes to her two robust globes. I, being accustomed to her beauty, was still not immune to its enticements, though. My mouth watered involuntarily. But I quickly recovered my bodily functions, put on a stone face, a mask like Sugar's. Then I sat.

Rochelle remained standing, arms folded under those gorgeous breasts. She stared and took in my appearance as a whole. Then slowly and deliberately, she sat on her money maker. "Damn, Mal, you look like shit," she commented.

"So, Rochelle, can't say I thought you would be the one waiting for me," I said.

"Malcolm, I am your wife. Of course you should—"

"Save it, Ro, Stop the false pretense."

Rochelle feigned shock. "What do you mean, Malcolm. I know this is hard for you, but attacking me is purely uncalled for," she said smoothly.

I leaned in closer to the Plexiglas, was tired of this verbal bullshit, this sparring with idle words. "Where the fuck have you been, Rochelle, hmmm?"

She got closer, mimicked my movement, got real close herself. "Been fucking one of your best friends," she whispered loud enough for me to hear. "Where the fuck have you been? Oh, yeah. That's right, you been sitting in this muthafucka cause you killed and fucked one of your best friends, too!" Her tone was saturated with the smugness she held toward me.

"Oh, well now at least you got your big girl panties on, so you going to throw that bullshit in my face, Ro? You believe that about me, Rochelle?"

"Doesn't matter what I believe, husband. Your transgressions have been plastered all over the news for the past few days. Perception is reality, Malcolm. You have compromised yourself and your family, and quite frankly, I refuse to let you bring down me and your children with you."

"I am curious, lover."

"About?"

"Did you think about this pussy at all when you and simple ass Sampson were sword fighting, or were you just focused on his hairy ass."

My eyebrow raised northward of its own accord, a reaction to my surprise of Rochelle's vulgarity.

"Well, Malcolm, are you going to answer me?"

I declined to answer, to even want to give any credence to her query.

"OK, husband, two more questions then."

I remained silent.

"Top or bottom? My guess, though Simple was the bigger of the two of you, is that you were on top. Am I right, Malcolm?"

"Rochelle, you need to stop," I whispered.

"Who sucked your dick better, husband, hmmm? Was it your wife or your fucking Magilla Gorilla lover?" she spat.

"Are you done? You said vows, Ro—took oaths before God. Now, when I need you the most, you going to what? Walk out and fuck Deke not even behind my back but in front of my goddamn face, using bullshit as your excuse!"

The guard on my side took a step forward. I raised my hands, palms open in a gesture of "my bad." He stepped back. Rochelle sucked in her teeth, made that annoying-ass sound. "Get mad all you want, Mal. You can't do shit for me in here, and besides, I had been hearing rumors about you and Simple Sampson for some time now. You may lie to everybody, even to yourself, but I know the truth, heard everything about your DL status from a very reliable source. I overlooked your many affairs, even let you talk me into swinging, but I have to draw the line somewhere, Malcolm."

"I didn't have to talk your freak nasty ass into anything,

Ro. As I recall, you enjoyed the swinging more than I did and what about your damn affairs. Those were all good, I guess."

"Am I the one in jail for murdering one of my lovers?" she teased.

That statement cut like a knife, didn't have much of a rebuttal for it. "I was framed, Rochelle. Someone is out to ruin my life, and I don't know why."

She looked as if she were about to explode with some truths, but held her tongue, remained composed and tight lipped. I observed her difficulty in maintaining that calmness. "You know something, don't you, Ro? Is it Black? Is Black out to get me?"

"What? Black? How would I know that, Malcolm? Black is family. I doubt if he would go after my husband you fool. He ain't even thinking 'bout your dumb ass." The street was seeping back into her reserved nature. "Stop trying to blame others for your shit, Mal. You put yourself here, and nobody else is to blame. I realize that now. Yes, I am fucking Deke. It's good, too, He attends to my needs, doesn't want or need a harem of women to satisfy his ego. I am more than enough for him."

"You were enough for me, Rochelle," I said deflated.

I lowered my head, couldn't believe the conversation had taken this turn.

Her face changed then, softened for the slightest of moments. She resembled my wife once more.

I said, "Rochelle, I don't care what you've done. I love you. I want us to get past all this crap, want to be a family again. I need you, baby."

"Malcolm—"Then as sudden as it came, it was gone. She was back to being the bitch instantly. Rochelle shook her head, looked to me as if she had just made a final decision. "How could you have been fucking Sampson behind my back, Mal? How could you?" Tears streamed down her beautiful face. She was becoming an emotional wreck.

"Rochelle, I didn't. I have done a lot of things, some of which you are aware of, but I chased skirts, baby. You know that. Who has told you otherwise? Who is filling your head with this nonsense? Who, Rochelle," I pleaded.

She refused to answer, just sat there and stared my way, tried to keep a nonchalant air about her. "It's over, Malcolm. We are through. I mean it this time. I know this isn't what you want to hear right now, but I have to get me and the boys off this sinking ship."

My mouth fell wide open, didn't expect this at all.

Then the anger came.

"Over!" I raged. "Over—what you gonna do for money, Miss Queen B, huh?" I continued. "You haven't worked in ages, so who is going to take care of your expensive-ass tastes."

That brought a smirk to her face. "Oh, you still will, honey, husband. I'm still your wife. Your ass is locked up. I control all our considerable assets now." She appeared even more relaxed, more confident. "I been waiting years for you to fuck up like this and now…well."

I exploded into motion, rushed forward, slapped the Plexi, made Rochelle flinch. "You money-loving bitch! You can't touch any of my fucking money!" I knew I spoke falsehoods, though.

Rochelle shook her head, wagged her index finger. "That's where you're wrong again, Mal. It's already mine, well, mine and your twin boys, even your substantial share in that whore house of yours...ah...Sugarland, is it? I got some plans and changes in mind for that place myself. Think it's time for a male stripper review in this town permanently."

By then, two behemoth guards had flanked me, had me subdued. My arms were pinned behind my back, with my head in some type of immobilizing hold. They could not restrain my vision, though, my red-seeing veiled eyes, locked them with my wife's.

She kissed two fingers, placed them against the glass. "Goodbye, Malcolm. I hope you fare well around all those hard dicks in there." Then she got up and strutted that beautiful ass away.

"Rochelle! Rochelle! Ro..chelllllllle!" I screamed till I was hoarse, and the guards, obvious pity in their hearts, allowed my verbal deflation to play out.

$ $ $

I barely recall returning to my cell. I knew I had to fight this despair, wanted to fight it, but didn't have the will, the energy to. Rochelle had just murdered my soul as surely as if she had shot me through the heart. I was prone on the uncomfortable bunk, had no strength to stand. But I had enough for one single gesture. I slid off the bunk, landed on the cold floor, made it to my knees, weakly got into position and prayed, wept and prayed, released all my frustrations and evils, let the holy come to take it all away.

Then without warning, I collapsed.

I awakened to shouting. At first, I couldn't discern what was being said but it sounded as if someone was being ordered around.

"Get him up off that hard-ass floor now please," the voice was female. I opened my eyes, was in a sitting position on my bunk. Fitz was in my cell with a guard and someone else.

Fitz grinned. "Boy, you got some friends in high places, Malcolm. Bail was set an hour ago. Let's get you out of here."

"Huh?" I turned, looked at the other presence in the cell, couldn't believe my eyes but there she stood, my salvation. She was as beautiful as ever.

Guess my prayers had been answered.

Sort of.

Deke   21

Night had fallen on my worries. I paced the floor of the hotel room I had acquired earlier, wasn't going back to my new house anytime soon, didn't trust I would leave there alive if I entered it. Black definitely had me spooked, which was what he had intended.

Damn!

I let that psycho force me from a home I had worked my ass off to get. I just didn't trust that weak bullshit Black was selling. For all I know, he could be getting out tomorrow, wanting me to feel a false sense of security for a few days. That was that cold muthafucka's way.

I at least had the chance to go by Sugarland, talk with Samantha, our more-than- competent manager. I told her to hold things down while I had some unexpected, out-of-town business, to handle. She had mentioned to me that Rochelle had been around a lot lately, that she had talked to her about some changes in the club. I told her to just humor

Ro. She was, after all, an owner and to just run any major changes by me first.

I didn't want or need any more drama, especially with Rochelle. I had planned on making a case for us. Yes, as crazy as it sounds, I was going to ask Rochelle to go away with me, to start a new life together. Shit, I would sell Sugarland. Malcolm wouldn't care. I'm sure he needed as much cash as he could muster for legal fees. No, he wouldn't care about the selling of the club, but he sure as hell would care if I left with his wife. I loved Malcolm. He had always been a brother to me, but nothing compares to the love a man has for a woman. Rochelle had always been the one for me, and now was my chance.

Black could fucking have Sugarland. I had my Sugar anyway. I think I had figured out how she pulled it off. Working only two days a week at Black's, made it possible for her, didn't know how she managed the change in voice though, but I was sure: Rochelle was Sugar. I was hoping to confront her tonight when she arrived at the hotel, hoped to get her to don the mask and fuck me the way Sugar had. Rochelle being Rochelle was freaky anyway, but she took it up a notch as Sugar. I grinned, didn't know why, had no reason to feel giddy. I had betrayed my best friend, lost another good friend to murder, and had a maniac wanting my head or my club. Yep, I had all the reasons in the world to be smiling, but thinking of being with Rochelle, with her in my bed…well…it dominated my thoughts. Lust is a powerful aphrodisiac.

I phoned Rochelle to see if I could coax her to bring that ass to me earlier, knowing full well that she wouldn't.

"Hello, what's going on, Dee? Have you been thinking about me, missing these lips. They been missing you."

"Hell, yeah. I been missing your fine ass all day, Ro," I practically yelled into the phone. "Why don't you come on over here earlier than we planned," I asked.

"No can do, lover. Still at my parents' farm in Mebane checking on the twins. They are having a tough time, what with their father being a jailbird now and all. This is a good place for them now, away from the madness."

"I understand," I lied. "Oh, by the way, I got a room at the Hilton right by the airport, so you don't have to drive all the way to Raleigh."

"That's sweet of you, baby. But, Deke. . ."

"Yeah..."

"Please refrain from telling me lies and feeding me bullshit," her voice grew aggravated.

"Huh, what do you mean, Rochelle?"

"I mean just tell me you hiding from Black and don't want to risk staying at your house, Deke."

I stood holding the phone in silence.

"Look, there's no shame in that. Black may be family to me but I know full well what he's capable of. Just keep it real with me, OK?."

"OK," I answered.

"No lies between us, is all I ask."

"Point made, Rochelle. See you later."

"Yes, you will, baby. Keep that thing hard for me."

I smiled. "Will do."

Rochelle   22

"Bye, baby…can't wait," I lied. Deke was beginning to become more of a damn problem, a freaking nuisance, than the distraction I had meant for him to be. The fool fell back in love with me just because I blessed him with some of this na-na. Damn shame. The nigga got pussy whipped so two-minute brotha quick.

Hell, I was still contemplating telling Black where his scared ass was hiding, but didn't want him taken out, not yet. Deke was a useful tool in my shed. Besides, I still wanted a little more of that devilish down stroke of his. He could roll them tight ass butt cheeks of his in a way that made me just cream and cream all over his shaft. And that fucking tongue—whew! Deke took that mouthpiece, made it dance, do the damn tango on my clit. Damn, I was making myself moist just thinking about it.

It was a fact. Malcolm may be bigger and a more forceful fuck, but Deke really enjoyed the pleasuring of my na-na. He feasted on cat like he had been starved for days, but he was gentle with it as well. That was a rare quality indeed in a man. It was just too bad he was lacking in some other areas, vital areas in my book.

Money.

Oh, sure, Deke was the force behind club Sugarland. No question that was his baby, and I must admit, he had turned that den of sin into a serious money maker; with my husband's money, though.

The simple fact was Black wasn't going to sit back, let shit ride, and not want his cut from Sugarland. They had stolen Sugar, or at least that's what he wanted everybody to believe. I never did, though, because I knew the truth. I grinned. That cousin of mine is something else. Shit, the only reason he hadn't moved in on them sooner, was because I was holding him back, pacifying him with money I was siphoning off. It wasn't enough, though. He wanted a share of their profits.

The greedy mofo wanted more than I could give without drawing attention to my manipulations of funds I had told Malcolm I needed for the family's daily expenses. Finally, I just told Black to do what he had to do to get Sugarland but just give me a little time. He agreed. Now was that time, I assumed. Sample had been eliminated, Malcolm was falling apart in a jail cell, and Deke wasn't shit without his two brothers, business wise at least. Of course, Black was going to take advantage of the situation now. Shit, that's just who he was, what he does. He would be especially cruel and swift once he knew I was done with Malcolm.

Malcolm! The damn fool couldn't get out of his own sexual deviant-ass way. We had rules, dammit! Rules that muthafucka willfully broke, had broken them with damn Sample, no less. I frowned, couldn't help the expression on my face when I thought of my husband and his secret lover.

I had been totally in the dark, clueless to the man I had shared a bed with, was totally unaware concerning his covert desires of the same sex. I had been stunned when his hidden lifestyle was made known to me.

Her name was Jennifer. She had been Sampson's lover, had shared many intimate encounters with him as I had with my husband. She would be my "Deep Throat," the harbinger of chaos, the fucking bearer of bad news. I'm not saying my marriage was perfect before I knew the truth, but it was safe for me, and I trusted Mal wouldn't break our rules.

He had.

After Jennifer told me her accounts of discovering Malcolm in bed with Sampson on more than one occasion, I began to take more notice of his comings and goings. Now it was true. I never really obtained any video or photos of Malcolm being with Sample or any man for that matter in any compromising positions, but that just meant his cheating ass was clever about his unsavory exploits, in my opinion.

What can I say. Jennifer was very convincing. She cried with every telling of her outlandish claims. Of course that meant nothing, I could turn on the waterworks display when I needed to as well. I just couldn't find a motive for her to bring a falsehood such as this to my life. She appeared hurt and devastated by what she saw, claimed to want a future with simple-ass Sampson. She wanted to have that fucker's babies. Ewww! She appeared to be a woman scorned, a woman protecting another woman.

We began to talk a lot after that initial meeting. We exchanged information readily...compared notes...bonded. I began to grow fond of this woman who was like a sister to me in this betrayal.

It was still a hard pill for me to swallow. I knew Malcolm loved pussy, and, well, truth be told, Simple-ass Sample was the only man to make my na-na squirt. Big horse-dick muthafucka! Deke hadn't even managed that even with his talented oral skills, came close though along with Mal.

Jen had stressed she saw the deed with her very own striking sky-blue eyes. Hard to argue with that. She had finally convinced me, then she seduced my panties right the hell off. I grinned. Yes, Jennifer was an excellent lover, one who I could see and hang with out in the open. Shit, we were just girlfriends after all.

Not!

Jennifer came to me one day with revenge on her mind. Didn't take much convincing on her part to get me to join her. I had dealt with a lot from my husband, and karma is a bitch. Wanted him to feel what I felt. I was on board as soon as she revealed her elaborate scheme. It might have seemed odd to some, that I could turn on my husband so easily, but his continuing infidelities and now this DL status was the catalyst for my involvement. Jen told me she needed specifically for me to obtain Malcolm's semen. I knew I could make that happen with relative ease, Mal being a sex fiend and all.

Actually, the opportunity came quicker than I anticipated. That night it was easy enough to get Mal's sperm. Shit, that Negro loves himself some head. I sucked his Adam damn near until he was in a coma that night, was the same night he hung out with his boys at Black's hole-in-the wall strip club.

I was adamant before I performed that he wear a condom. Told him I knew he fucked one of those nasty-ass stripper hos. He argued, but let me put one on. Then I just held onto his baby-makers till Jen called me for them.

Still, I didn't know how Jen pulled off the fingerprints on the syringe though. Somehow she did, and now I was on the verge of getting it all. It worked better than I could have expected. The police had no clue. Nobody suspected us or a frame job, to be honest. Besides, even if they did, Sample's crooked ass had made many enemies on the street.

It surprised me how easily I handled the whole situation. I was numb to the murder, numb to my husband being falsely imprisoned for it. Shit, it was Malcolm's own fucking fault. He had my love, had my total trust once, had all of me and didn't fully appreciate the woman I was. My kitty wasn't enough for him. That hardened me, turned my heart cold. He always seemed to need more.

I was on the edge of tears thinking of my marriage. I had truly loved Malcolm. He was the father of my beautiful children, was my rock at one point, but that love dissolved like sugar into water the minute I learned of his ultimate betrayal. Just didn't care anymore.

I was on my way to club Sugarland before meeting up with Deke to set up that male review event with Samantha. We were thinking of trying it out this weekend. Had to interview some local talent to go with some out-of-town performers.

Shee-it! I like to think I'm a good judge of dick! Samantha, the club manager, was turning into my biggest supporter. I knew she had been hired by Deke, but we were of like minds on a lot of possibilities concerning Sugarland. She no longer viewed me as an outsider. Basically, I liked that bitch.

Maybe the two of us could partner up once the smoke cleared and open up our own club. I could definitely get behind a project like that, would have Black's blessing if I chose to go that route. I couldn't or wouldn't take Sugar as Deke and the others had, though. Her ass would have to retire with the closing of Sugarland.

It was something to think about. But first I would have to do something about Deke, maybe convince him to leave Durham, hell, North Carolina even. He needed to start over somewhere new and fresh. If he didn't have the money for the move, I'd give it to him. Probably owed him that much, just from the multiple orgasms alone. Leaving might be the only way to save his life! It would also solve my potential problem with his lovesick ass.

Yes, I could feel a plan formulating in my head now, and after I dealt with him, then it would be Jennifer's turn.

So much to do, so little time.

Sugar   23

I had to take off the mask, the contacts, had to allow the other to do the job that needed doing. She performed to perfection. I was pleased, was prideful of her confidence, but now Sugar had to take control, had to do some dirty deeds that I was the master of. I'm not saying she wasn't a sexual creature as well. She actually had learned a lot since the two of us had been together. I was the proud parent when I experienced my offspring's performances. She had learned well from me, and I could tell she wanted to show me she could accomplish this task as well. She wanted the pleasure of it, thought she would fight me for the control. Instead, I relented it to her, for now.

As I said, I retreated just far enough to let the more reserved one take over for a bit. She allowed me to be present as she negotiated our little pawn's release.

It was I, Sugar, who gave her the ammunition to persuade and force the hand of the Honorable Judge Steven

Thomas to grant a suitable bail. You see, Mrs. Thomas had no earthly idea of her assumed faithful and upstanding husband's affinity for ah...how shall I say...masked strippers. I knew eventually his secret liaisons with me would pay dividends.

After liberating Malcolm, we decided it would be best to acquire a room rather than let him retire to his home. No sense in alerting anyone to his presence too soon. I was just thankful he had agreed.

We watched him now. I could feel her arousal growing with my own, felt the tingle in our loins, the desire turning to heat, morphing into a raging fire, making our skin glisten with a coat of sweat.

We watched.

Now he slumbered peacefully on the leather sofa in this spacious and luxurious hotel room. Nothing but the best for this man. Sure, it was a stark contrast to his more recent accommodations. We observed him sleep for awhile, marveled at the rise and fall of his nicely chiseled chest. It was erotic, hypnotizing even. Yes, we wanted this man, wanted him to seed our fertile crop. Had plans that would make things all the sweeter if we could coax the creamy satisfaction from his loins. We understood he craved a release. We just had to be the instrument of it.

We could have had him freed days ago, but it wasn't the right time then. He wasn't seasoned enough for our liking at the time, still held most of his sanity. He had to squirm just a bit longer, would make his gratitude for us all the more appetizing.

This was probably the first decent rest he had managed

in days. We climbed on the sofa, straddled his almost-lifeless form, unbuttoned his shirt, pulled his slacks, boxers, and socks off. He stirred a little due to our disrobing making him feel his nakedness.

We admired it, his beautiful muscled frame, that edible generous member of his. We covered his exposed tantalizing flesh with a sheet, then stepped out of our dress and padded toward the bathroom.

At some point, the clock on the wall near the bathroom was noticed. Still had a few hours to kill. I knew how I wanted that time occupied when I glimpsed Malcolm beginning to pitch a tent while he slept.

She agreed.

I grinned. Yes, I had a few hours to kill.

The hotel bathroom was as large as some homes' master bedrooms, had one of those sunken tubs, looked like a mini pool with those Jacuzzi jets. I leaned over, breasts heaving and swaying, then turned the faucet on to fill the tub. I had purposefully let the bathroom door stay ajar, anticipating that the high volume of running water would wake Malcolm. Wanted him to wake and then investigate.

After the water was at a steaming sufficient level, I lowered my already combustible body into more heat. It was soothing, though. I soaped my flesh, spread my legs wide, let one of the water jets molest me. I used a finger to aid it, closed my eyes, got lost in the sensations.

The fire burned.

The lust for flesh would not be extinguished.

We opened our eyes to the site of Malcolm standing in the doorway, very nude and very aroused.

"You just going to stand there gawking," we said. "Come and join. The water is…ah…just fine." I retreated back then, let her take the lead. Wanted to see how she would ravish him.

Malcolm stared, had the look of a thirsty man surrounded by others drinking. He came to the tub without hesitation, lowered himself into the heat, the tub and ours.

"I needed this," he admitted. "Thank you."

"You don't have to keep thanking me, Malcolm," I said. "Well, not with your words anyway." I raised a soap-covered leg his way. He needed no other gesture, took the initiative then.

Malcolm became somewhat amphibian. He ducked his head beneath the soapy water, found my clit with his mouth, parted my submerged skins and licked. Licked and sucked like he had the ability to breathe underwater. My thighs were quivering though they were partially underneath the warm water. My long legs were outstretched, Malcolm's head buried between them. I felt the rise in my belly, knew the tide was increasing as it gathered momentum. Malcolm raised his head, inched closer to my face, stopped to suckle on my breasts, each given its own personal attention. I was through, was in a tub full of water but was wetter than that. My own juices flowed uncontrollably; I came so violently, so brutal, couldn't keep from screaming, ever increasing the volume to my pleasure. Damn!

Malcolm continued his sexual journey upward, found my face, smiled, covered my mouth with his own. He invaded my mouth with his tongue, snaked it around mine, explored the humid cavern my tongue resided in with his own. His technique was beautiful. It was amazing. It made her shiver.

I felt her falling, drifting into the madness an apex lover could pull you into. She relented to him, opened herself up, dare I say, started to make love to him.

No!

I regained control then, pushed her back, to watch, to feel, to see how it's done. I had to prove to her it was Eve who ruled Adam, made him do her bidding. She, we were superior!

I tongued Malcolm back furiously, grabbed his face, licked around his lips, smiled. I told him, "Let's get in that big-ass-bed in there."

He nodded, followed my lead, and toweled me dry. I took his hand into my mine and led him to the bed, took some of the complimentary oils from the bathroom and rubbed him down with them. One had the scent of jasmine. It seeped into his pores, its fragrance turning the both of us on even more.

Malcolm was on his back looking up. I went to him then, straddled his body, put him inside with a gasp. He was not average, but I would accommodate his size. I sat still for a lingering moment, enjoying his length, his girth, the sensation of being filled. I never tire of it, always searched for its presence. When found, had to take the time to savor the feeling. I tilted my head back, closed my eyes, got tight around his sin, squeezed gently at first, then I made a fist around his Adam.

"Aaaaaah…," I moaned. My ass was spread wide this

way. I loved this position, had total control over cums, his and ours. Malcolm reached around me, had two cheeks for his two hands. He tried to guide me, tried to control that which couldn't be. I locked gazes with him, shook my head, took his hands and placed them over his head, held them pinned there while I rode. I churned my ample hips as I rode, swayed to a rhythm in my head, rolled to a perfect harmony with his upward thrusts.

Yes!

I let loose the snapper!

That hidden ability that only a few blessed sexually omnipotent women possess, was as rare as a foot- long man. Sure they were real, but were also scarce. So was the mythical snapper, could make a normal man come in seconds. I reserved its use for special occasions, this being one.

Malcolm was no ordinary man, though, could tell he had had snapper before. He controlled his orgasm, refused to cum.

I rode harder, churned, and rolled slowly when I could feel his tip, then milked him while I let my ass fall to his lap.

"Oh God—oh shit!" he screamed.

I smiled devilishly, knew I had him then, knew the involuntary clenching and unclenching of my sugar walls had started his chain reaction. I saw his muscles tighten, took note of his fuck face...damn... even that was handsome, pretty muthafucka!

"Aaaargh!" He bellowed like a bear as his release took hold of him. I could feel him splashing my insides, could feel his hot voluminous liquid filling me. It sent us over the edge, we—yes we dammit came as one, came like never before. It was strange, but this was the first threesome we had been a part of.

It would not be the last.

When our spasms of climax finally subsided, I collapsed on top of him, still managed to hold him inside; was still clenching and unclenching. He kissed me violently, ravenous in his afterglow. He surprised me, didn't think any man could recover from such an explosion so soon. Malcolm was no ordinary man.

"Damn, Mal, you were only locked up for a week," I managed.

"Felt longer to me, though," he said with lust hanging on every word.

"Down, boy. Save some for later, OK? I have to get a shower and make this meeting."

"Who are you meeting with in the middle of the night?" he inquired.

"Someone that might help with your case and something I got going on," I answered.

He didn't look convinced but ceased his questioning. Think that powerful orgasm was finally kicking in. I kissed him gently, got off of him, broke the connection, bent down, kissed the head of his dick, then strolled to the shower - the embodiment of Eve.

$ $ $

I left Malcolm in a deep slumber. I knew he would be comatose until morning. Now, Sugar was in full control. Let the other have her fulfillment with Malcolm, but now, Sugar had to take care of business. It was time to bring all our plans to a head, time to execute and move on.

As I drove to my destination, I searched and found the right mood music on the radio. I found Tupac's "Shed So Many Tears" and sang along as I cruised.

It wasn't going to be easy, this part of my plan, but it had to be done. I exited my vehicle, walked to the front door of this familiar house, in this familiar neighborhood, and rang the bell. I shifted my weight from one foot to the other as I waited. Nervous…I was nervous! She opened the door wearing red French-cut panties and a mid-length Durham Police Department t-shirt.

Watts said, "Come in, Shugah." She eye raped me as she rushed me, tongued the hell out of me, tasting toothpaste and residuals of Malcolm, I'll bet.

"Hey, Watts. I brought some Dirty H2O for after."

"After what?"

"After we fuck, of course," I said.

She smiled, hugged me tight, then closed her front door, and led me further into her domicile.

I sat on her Italian leather couch, made myself as comfortable as I could, and relaxed. Wanted her to do and feel the same. I patted the cushion next to me for her to join me on the chair.

"We're almost there, baby. Now it's time for you to meet up with the bitch and turn up the heat."

"Oh, when?"

"Tonight," I answered.

"Tonight?" she asked perplexed.

"Yeah, send a text and tell her to meet you at club Sugarland after it closes."

"Sugarland? Why meet there? Surely we can just have her come over here or something."

"Don't be stupid, Watts."

"Sugarland is neutral territory. It may be a den of sin, but it's still a public place. Even after hours, you shouldn't draw much attention to yourselves. You can take my car."

"OK, baby. I'll set up the meeting," Watts cooed.

"Now, Watts," I demanded. She took a long hard look at me. Obviously she didn't appreciate my tone, but I had to get her to understand the magnitude of meeting tonight.

"What should I say?"

"Just tell her to meet you in a couple of hours and that it's extremely important."

"What if she can't—"

"Make her, Watts. Come up with something. Damn, you fucking her. I'm sure you can use that to your advantage."

"OK, OK," she whined.

Watts picked up her phone and began to text. I took the liberty to roam her flesh, caressed her thighs with gentle hands as well as tongue. Wanted her mind to be flooded with visions of Sugar. I needed her occupied with making me happy and wanting some reward for her good behavior. She knew I could satisfy her like no other, that I would always pacify her with sexual gratification if she did my bidding. I was Watts's addiction, her drug of choice. She was an addict strung out on Sugar, and the problem for her was Sugar knew it. So I gave her a little appetizer and waited for her subsequent moans.

"Do you want this done or not," she said in breathy tones.

I answered by pulling those red-laced panties off of her, took one finger and made circles on her clit. "Make it happen, Watts. Then I'll make this...uh...happen," I breathed into her ear.

I made my tongue roll, made ripples appear like waves disturbing calm water. Then I placed it on her sex.

"Done," she moaned. "She'll come...she...agreed...couple...oooh...h-hours."

"Excellent," I said. "It looks like we got a little time to kill before you have to leave."

"Uh-uh..."

I got more aggressive then, nestled my head between the toned but soft flesh of her thighs, tasted her sugar. Watts was sweet, had an agreeable flavor to my palate. I devoured her like it was my last meal, like I would miss this for a lifetime.

"Shugah! Shu...gah!" Watts squealed in delight. She was a loud lover. That turned some on. Me, it just validated this wicked tongue of mine. I wanted her to have the climax of all climaxes and I ate her na-na to orchestrate that ending.

It didn't take long for Watts to comply. "Oh—fuck! Gaaaaad!" She gushed all in my mouth, tasted like peaches, I smiled. Mission accomplished.

I left Watts lounging on the couch, left her with a

"Kool-Aid" grin on her face, entered her kitchen which was familiar to me. I had been here many times. I found her blender on the marble countertop and mixed up her favorite drink.

I heard Watts humming a beautiful melody and joined her with my own voice over the sound of the blender. We hummed in harmony, if there was such a thing.

Watts and I had such a connection. We were more than mere lovers. There existed between us a real sisterhood, a meeting of the minds. I smiled as I thought about the many experiences we had shared over the years.

"Watts...Jennifer, I got your favorite."

"You said Jennifer. You never use my first name." She looked giddy. "Sounded sexy coming from your lips, though,"

"Really...could've sworn I've used it before but if you say so. Which do you prefer?"

"Whatever you want to call me is OK by me, babe," she said taking the drink.

I sat in the crook of the sofa, my back in the corner. Watts sat between my legs, her head resting against my chest.

I breathed the scent of her shampoo as I rested my chin atop her head, the fragrance being citrus. She rubbed my bare thighs, continued to sip her drink.

"These moments are precious to me, Shug. We've come a long way since Georgia, sister."

"Yes, seems like a lifetime ago. Thank God the Institute gave me at least one thing positive."

Watts turned, looked me in the face. "I love you,

Shugah. You know that, right? I've done all of this for you…for your sanity. I hope when this is over, you can finally have some peace."

I looked at her, didn't see the" her" of today, though. Saw her as she was all those years ago when we first met. She was just a skinny little runt then, small in stature but big in heart. She had my back on too many occasions to count, I mused. Watts always had those hypnotic eyes of hers even back then. I recall being intrigued by them. We had looked out for one another since day one.

The Institute was part prison, part psych ward. It was for women with issues, big issues. Because of the gang mentality of its patients/prisoners, Watts and myself coupled up for survival. She was my anchor for such a long period of time back then.

Now was different.

Time changes people, changes them sometimes for the better, sometimes for the worse. Time hadn't done its thing on us as a union, but had changed me as an entity. I existed in Gemini form, was born under that zodiac sign as well. I was "we" now.

I watched Watts gulp down the last of her Dirty Water, did so and licked her lips, savoring the taste.

"Damn, Shug. You out did yourself on that one. It tasted sweeter than usual. Did you put some essence of Sugar in there?" she joked.

I gave the back of her head serious eyes. "Not quite. Want another?"

"Sure, baby."

She raised herself, allowed me to move from

underneath her, our naked bodies stuck to the leather. Watts patted my bottom as I walked by. I retrieved the other pre-made drink and handed it to her, then kissed her with all the passion and feelings I felt coursing through my veins.

I cupped her face in my hands. "I love you too, Jen."

She grinned, looked a little tipsy.

"You drunk, Watts," I stated more than asked.

"Nah—not yet." She downed that one with two gulps. I returned to my prior position behind her, fondled her still-erect nipples. then I massaged her shoulders.

The first sign came in the form of nausea, then severe abdominal pains.

"Shug, I…I don't feel well." Watts fell off the sofa, landed on the floor terribly hard. She screamed in pain, grabbed at her stomach.

"Aaaaargh!" she yelled. "Help me, Shugah…h-h-help." Her voice grew weaker by the second. Watts's skin took on an unhealthy hue.

I was surprised by the rapidness of the drink. I came to her slowly, tears already cascading in bountiful amounts.

Watts managed a fetal position. She was in such pain. "Whaza—what did you do to me, Shug." Her voice was very faint now. I approached with a calmness I didn't feel. This was my bitch, my right hand, and I had done this to her.

"I'm sorry, Jen. It has to be this way. This is your final gift to me. This will help in securing my sanity."

Her eyes bulged. Yes, there was the presence of the physical pain, but I could tell it was more of the mental variety. Watts scrutinized me up and down with total shock, then with recognition.

"You…y-you…still love you, Shugah," she whispered.

I turned and wept, hoped she wouldn't suffer like this much longer. "She" took over then, was horrified by what I had done but she wasn't without approval. She never really embraced Watts, had viewed her as more adversary than colleague. She thought I had grown too close to Watts. Then she stood over her body. Watts was still cramped up, still in a fetal position.

She smiled. I in turn mimicked her gesture.

She forced my smile aimed at Watts.

Damn!

We were becoming one.

Watts was beyond communicating now. All she could do was moan. Now she moaned in pain. Just minutes prior she had moaned in bliss. Life can change so swiftly in that regard.

From sugar to shit…is what some say.

I was in control again, wiped my face with the back of my hand. I placed one last kiss on Watts's forehead then went about the task of wiping my presence from this place.

I reached into my duffel bag and pulled the items that I had packed to take care of this job. I placed the latex gloves on my hands, pulled out a Tyvek full-body disposable hazmat suit. Most people use them for cleaning up hazardous waste. I figured it would serve its purpose in my clean up.

I wiped my prints off of everything I had ever touched in that house, which wasn't much. Watts preferred to rendezvous in hotel rooms for the simple "different factor" of things. Being in assorted hotels spiced up our sex life. As if our sex needed spice, but it's what she liked, which benefited me now.

After cleaning my prints from top to bottom, I vacuumed thoroughly from room to room, carefully vacuumed the sofa as well.

I went to her bedroom, fished through her private belongings. Knew Watts had to have kept some personal mementos of the past. I was sorry I had to violate her this way, but I had to destroy any link between the two of us.

Eventually I came across a shoebox marked "Georgia." In it, were old pictures of me and Jennifer. Even in those days, we hardly smiled. I noticed that point immediately. She had several photos of us as teens, then as women. Photos of a more sexual nature as well. She had letters I had written her, still had business cards from the first strip club the both of us worked in Atlanta. The memories started to flood my mind then. The good times, the sharing, the uncompromising love she had for me, gave me pause. What have I fucking done! I sat and had a good cry for a moment, wasn't blubbering or anything like that but the water was definitely flowing. I became WE again. My resolve along with my strength returned. Time to finish this!

After I wept, I got myself together and took everything in the box, including the box itself. I found just one more item that could have linked the two of us. It was one of my first masks that I had given her. Took that, too, and placed it inside the box. Satisfied, I went back to Watts.

She was still but remained breathing at a shallow level.

I was thankful her face was no longer contorted in the pain, wracked expression she held earlier. She basically had blacked out. I knew her organs were shutting down, knew her fight to live was almost over.

I took a deep breath, calmed myself, and grabbed Watts by her ankles and dragged her to her bathroom. I was thankful she lived in a single-floor home. Would've been hell negotiating stairs with her dead weight. As it was, I got her into the shower, sat her at the end of the tub and turned on the shower head. Watts had one of those detachable shower heads, so I took it off, washed and rinsed her as thorough as I could. That task accomplished, I left her in a seated position with the water running. It would aid in the ridding of any of my remaining DNA.

I had one more chore to do, the most important part of this plan as a matter of fact.

I went to Watts's laptop and began to compose her final words as I saw them. She would ensure my plans would go off without a hitch with her sacrifice. I knew that a suicide letter that wasn't handwritten would be viewed skeptically, but counted on this age of email and text messaging to override that.

If I succeeded, it would come off very convincing and cover my tail in the telling.

I left Watts's home quietly in the night, overwhelmed with emotions. "Rest in peace, Jen," I said. "You will have some company very soon."

I drove toward Sugarland for a meeting and a killing. Looked at my watch. Damn, making good time as usual. Tonight I was going to finish my business in Durham.

Besides, Watts had fulfilled one more task for me that was crucial to the master plan. She supplied me with pertinent intelligence on Uncle Sam's bitch.

He would wait for now.

I cracked a grin. Revenge is sweet indeed.

Sugar is sweeter.

Rochelle   24

Me and Samantha had a good time with the interviews. I had this one bull who was absolutely gorgeous, had tried to get me to come home with him. His stage name was Pipelayer, and, whew, I just knew he could lay some pipe with those gyrations he displayed in his mouth- watering routine. Fuck, that Negro even went totally naked for us. I told him he didn't need to but didn't really dissuade him from doing so. Pipelayer owned more than a foot of dick while soft.

While fucking soft!

He had us measure him with a tape measure, Sam almost lost it. I on the other hand took the lead and signed him for the review. His real name was Calvin. I knew I would see Calvin at some point outside of the club 'cause I personally wanted to see if I could handle all that damn dick.

Damn! I couldn't stop thinking about it! Wasn't

thinking so much about Calvin the man, was more about his thick-ass dick. Though, Calvin himself was easy on the eyes: around six feet four, a good 225 of chiseled body, had a honey-wheat skin tone with light green eyes and a smooth (bump free) shaved head. He was BDGS - Big Dick and Gorgeous Smile.

So basically, he was a no brainer. His movements as he performed were those of a supremely talented lover. I could tell he had probably curled more toes than Idaho curled fries as he unleashed that monster on the unsuspecting public.

I fanned my face with my hand, had the A/C on full blast to no avail. That Negro had me shook. Had to get myself composed before I arrived at the hotel to meet up with Deke. I was going to rock his damn world something fierce before I sent him packing.

It was hard to drive with my panties being as wet as they were. Shit, I had a brush fire raging down there, couldn't get to that hotel quick enough. It was going to be a good night, cause I planned on busting a minimum of three nuts—guess Malcolm didn't realize the monster he had created with his deviant ass ways.

Deke had left instructions at the front desk to supply me with a key so I could let myself in (thoughtful mofo), and as I did so, I could hear the faint but distinct sounds of slumber coming from the nearly dark room. He had left the television on, looked as if he was watching "skin-a-max," with his horny ass. One of those cheap-ass soft porn flicks was on the screen. How anybody would want to watch simulated fucking rather than the real thing was beyond me.

My feeling is, if I'm going to watch porn, well dammit, I better see some dick slamming into some twat, but I digress.

I approached Deke. He still hadn't stirred much, hadn't sensed my presence yet. He was clothed in nothing but a white towel that was semi wrapped around his lower torso. Must have fallen asleep after taking a shower, I figured.

I gently moved the towel so that he was lying in all his glory. Deke was a very good looking man. I had to admit it. He wasn't a pretty boy like Malcolm, but was handsome in a thuggish, sexy kind of way. He owned a well-defined frame, a nice chiseled physique as well, had a coffee with cream kind of hue with perfect lips and teeth. That smile of his probably dropped more panties for him than his nice body.

Deke had charm as well, could talk to you as a friend. I just wished he would have turned out to be the successful one, rather than the struggling one. I sighed. Oh, well. It is what it is.

I got up, left a trail of clothes as I strolled to the bathroom, took a quick shower, returned to my concubine naked while he continued to slumber. I decided instantly how I would awaken "sleeping beauty." Couldn't contain my smile. Was one of pure sexual intent, one of fiendish desire.

Deke lay almost dead-like as I climbed on the bed and maneuvered my head just inches from his head, the brainless one. I licked the tip, circled his mushroom using my tongue to probe every delicious inch of his good bar. He moaned then, his eyes began to flutter, ready to open. I gave him heat then, let him feel the humidity of my mouth, was going to gift Deke with some sloppy head tonight. I bobbed up and then all the way down on his wood, allowed my gag reflex to take hold, made my mouth so saturated that way. Deke was wide awake now, calling my name, no longer moaning it. I must admit, I love the way men howl and squirm due to a skilled head doctor. He was my puppet while I held his dick in my humid prison. It glistened with my saliva, looked like he had cum already but that was my own soppy fluid. I wrapped tongue around his shaft as I bobbed. This was a practiced art. I had put in years of quality BJs to get to this upper level of skill, and Deke was the current recipient of all my hard work, of all that time well spent.

He lost his battle, the mind over the orgasm. The orgasm won. It didn't matter to me, though, I wanted his explosion to come swifter than usual. His bliss was thick, kind of tangy in taste, was rather pleasant as it flowed down my throat. I milked him dry, milked him limp, raised my head and shared his own taste with him as we tongue wrestled for a bit.

We then switched positions: me on my back, his head between my thighs. He opened me up with his thick fingers, invaded and probed my sex with that snake-like tongue of his. I just put my head back and let wave after body-shaking wave roll over me, put me in an out-of-body state.

I vaguely remembered my voice, just recalled the many levels of moans I made. Deke made me scream so much I grew hoarse, had me squealing so high I was sure I reached dog whistle heights.

Earlier, I had said I was on a quest for at least three cums, Deke had me at number four within the hour.

Damn that tongue!

We lay in bed then, hand in hand, both orally satisfied. Lay there until our breathing slowed, became literally in sync with one another. I crawled onto his chest, rested my head there, listened to his heartbeat, its rhythm almost put me to sleep.

Almost.

"Deke," I said. "We have to talk."

"Don't know that I like the way you said that, Ro."

"Look." I lifted my head, held his gaze with my own. "Black's not playing around. You need to get out of Durham. You really need to leave North Carolina. period."

He smiled at me. Was it really going to be this easy? "Great minds think alike, baby. I was thinking that very same thing. We can sell the club, give Malcolm his cut, and relocate somewhere nice, maybe a warm weather climate. How's Florida sound?"

I gave the fool a look as if he suddenly grew a second head or some other deformity. He eyed my expression closely, studied it. I knew he was waiting on my next words. I had to choose them carefully.

"I told you, Deke, you need to leave. As much as I would like to run away with you, I have a family here. My sons love this area. They never really cared to live in DC like Malcolm wanted. I can't leave, at least not right now."

He stood, paced the floor in front of the bed. His face was covered with the image of pure rage. "So you fuck me and dump me? Is that it, Ro? I know you got kids. Hell, I'm their uncle and godfather, for Christ sake, but with what we have growing, we…"

"What we have. Deke, let's get something straight. We've been having great mind-blowing sex. I love the way you pay attention to my needs, but I'm a married woman, Dee. I'm married to your best friend no less, and you can't expect me to just up and leave with you. There are things that have to be done first." I regretted the statement as soon as it slipped from my lips.

Deke gazed at me with hope then. "So you saying I should leave now and you would come later." His smile returned. "I could secure us a home somewhere, pave the way for you to follow later."

I shook my head. "No, Dee, I'm not totally closing the door on that possibility, but it won't be as quick as you are suggesting."

I have to decide what to do about my marriage, my new home, how my boys would take leaving the state with their father locked up here. I have to consider all these things. Actually, I just want you to leave, to be safe, Dee. You crossed Black with opening that club. I know it was your dream, but you've been around him long enough to know there would be a price to pay."

"Fuck Black!" he screamed. "Fuck that punk ass muthafucka! He don't scare me, Ro!"

"He should," I whispered." He may be my fam' but I know what he will do to you and, Dee—"

"Yeah…"

"I don't want that for you. You were my first love.

Listen to me, if you want to sell the club…well, fine. If you want to keep it and run it through me, that's OK, too."

He raised his brow in contemplation. "It takes money to pick up and move, Rochelle. I just got a fucking house in Raleigh. What am I supposed to do with that?"

"I'll help you. I have some assets at my disposal, enough to give you a new start elsewhere. Hey, hear me out on this."

"OK…"

"Why don't you sell me your share of the club. I'll give you a more than fair price, then you don't have to worry about Black taking or burning it to the ground. And if for any reason you want back in, I'll sell you your share back, at a profit of course. How's that sound?"

"So Sugarland would be yours free and clear, huh? What's to stop you from selling it then?"

"I won't. I promise, Deke." I hoped I sounded sincere. "I know this is not what you want to hear, baby, but take this way out, please."

He studied my face again. Silence existed between us for a few moments. It was broken by the all-too-familiar sound of a vibrating cell phone. Mine.

I had just received a text message from Jennifer asking to meet me at Sugarland later.

Strange.

I had forgotten Deke was scrutinizing me with cold eyes as I glanced at my phone. "Who's that?" he asked with jealousy seeping into his tone.

"It's nothing, just my mom asking about my mac-n-cheese recipe."

He read lie all over my face but decided not to press me on the issue. "OK, Rochelle, let's come up with a fair figure and do this."

"I'll discuss this with Fitz and have him draw up some papers ASAP, OK?"

"Fine."

"I'm going to grab a shower now. Care to join me?"

"In a minute, OK?" he said taking a seat on the bed. I left him alone, alone with his thoughts. He was also alone with my phone.

I could tell as I left Deke, he was more than a little agitated. He never joined me in the shower. Didn't matter to me, though, I had been thoroughly satisfied by that wicked tongue of his. Shit, he had me looking like a damn DUI suspect. Legs were still shaky. He had got some bomb-ass head from me as well, though, so I figured all's well that ends well.

My mind drifted to Jennifer. Why did she need to meet with me and more importantly, were we still in the clear concerning Malcolm's set-up. She had been so adamant about us keeping a low profile.

I had to admit, I was a bit apprehensive about meeting her at the club late at night, but she made it sound extremely important that we touch base.

I just hope, Jen wasn't horny, 'cause as I stated before, this kitty-cat's appetite had been sated. Jen could be a very demanding lover, and I just wasn't up for it after my tryst with Deke. I was a sexaholic as much as the next bitch, but, damn, Deke had left his name in my cat.

I pulled into the BP off of 70, didn't want to but was

forced to stop and fill up. I couldn't find my purse. Damn, must have left it at the hotel with Deke. Luckily I kept a stash of cash in my glove box, so I went inside to prepay.

When I approached the front door, it opened for me. Standing there holding it with a big- ass grin on his handsome mug, was none other than the Pipelayer himself, Calvin.

"Well, well, well, if it isn't the lovely Miss Lee," he said with his eyes roaming my frame.

"Hi, Calvin, and that's Mrs. Lee," I corrected.

"Oh, my bad. Mrs. Lee, what are you doing out this late?"

"Excuse me?"

"I just meant I wouldn't let my beautiful woman be out late at night getting gas alone."

"How do you know I'm alone," I asked.

"Saw you pull up and quite frankly, I said a silent prayer that you would be—"

"Why's that," I teased.

"Cause you know I'm trying to get some quality time with you." His confidence showed then. "Let's go somewhere and…ah…talk."

"Talk, huh?"

"Talk or whatever you like." He gave me that pretty-boy smile that always seems to weaken my knees and soak my panties. Shit, Calvin was F-I-N-E, and what's more, he knew it!

I glanced at my watch, still had some time to kill before Jen was to meet me. I must be crazy thinking what I was thinking, but I hadn't had any dick tonight and dammit, I wanted to see if I could take that monster Calvin had jailed in his pants. I didn't want to risk him seeing Jen, though.

"I have to meet someone at the club now, but maybe…"

"Don't say later, Rochelle. Let me follow you over, make sure you're safe, then I'll leave when whoever you're meeting shows up." He made a cross-my-heart gesture. "Promise."

"Calvin, I…I don't know." I could hear and detect the waver in my own voice as I spoke. He could as well.

"Come on, Rochelle, you know you want to. This could be our night. I know you're curious."

"Curiosity killed the cat," I said.

"Or in your case, could fill the cat."

I smiled, he smiled. "You are so sure of yourself, huh?"

"Confident, not cocky, though. Well, maybe a bit cocky."

I gave him the once over again. He had on a black tank with black linen pants. Defined muscles covered his entire young body. Besides, this dumb fuck didn't know anything and what was he going to say even if he saw Jennifer.

"OK, follow me," I said.

Calvin couldn't contain his smile. I was glad he couldn't, made him that much more attractive. He walked me back to my car, pumped my gas, and followed me to Sugarland.

Deke 25

I paced the floor still full of rage. Who does that bitch think she's dealing with. I must have "Boo-boo the fool" tattooed on my forehead. So Rochelle thinks she can discard me like a used tampon and I should just go away quietly.

Fuck!

Why do I love the bitch so much?

When Rochelle was showering, of course I looked at her damn cell phone, saw the text message that some fool had left her. She was to meet this person at Sugarland no less! I got the sense that it was an important meeting of the two, and that they knew each other intimately.

I needed to calm down before I did something rash. I decided to sit for a minute and roll me a blunt to think. Soon, I was puffing and calming, was surprisingly able to think about things more clearly as I inhaled the smoky relaxation. Things began to come into focus quite rapidly.

Rochelle was playing me for a fool, had used me to hurt Malcolm. She had planned to screw me and really screw him the whole time since Mal's incarceration. I had simply been the instrument of her revenge on him. I wasn't quite sure what Malcolm had done to spark such a twisted, scorned woman, but I could well guess infidelity had to be at the core. Malcolm enjoyed a variety of women. Maybe Rochelle had finally snapped, finally had enough of his adulterous ways. I guess she decided to drag my lovesick ass into their drama because she knew I still held a torch for her affections. She understood I never really had gotten over their marriage, and she used my feelings against me.

Bitch!

I still fumed. Now it was in measured fury. I decided to make a trip to Sugarland myself. But first I had a stop to make. I wasn't going unarmed, and I wasn't going to be no damn fool about things.

Black could be waiting on me to show up there or at the very least, he could have one of his lackeys on the lookout for me. I was willing to take the chance. I knew I was being foolish, but my heart wouldn't allow me to not confront Rochelle. I just hoped I wouldn't regret this decision.

Somebody was going to give me some fucking answers one way or the other.

Malcolm   26

I opened my eyes to darkness. It was difficult to move, felt like someone was sitting on my chest. I was still feeling the effects of that all-consuming orgasm that I had. I hadn't cum like that in some time, could barely focus on any one thing in the room.

"Stacy. Stacy are you here?" Silence greeted my query. I felt alone because I was alone. Stacy must've left for her meeting. I put my hands behind my head, eyes were looking upward, wasn't anything to see but darkness, so I closed them to think.

To say I was shocked when Stacy showed up in my cell with Fitz was a huge understatement. Considering how we parted the last time we were in each other's company, I would have assumed she would be cheering on the prosecutor with pompoms raised. Stacy must hold no grudges toward me. I guess she blamed Rochelle for what she had to endure that night in the office. I could tell she still had feelings for me.

Stacy had appeared as my guardian angel, an angel with a devilish shape. Damn, the way that woman moved in the throes of passion was just amazing. Almost like she danced on the dick! It was like she moved to her own personal erotic rhythm and I was just along for the ride.

Then…all of a sudden…something clicked.

I pictured Stacy as she rode me into an explosive climax, was remembering her sexual movements, her dance of sin on my pole. I recalled another with those same moves, those similar gyrations.

Sugar!

No way! I must be high or something. But the more I thought about it, the more my imaginations ran wild. Could I really be right about them? Maybe, just maybe…

That was it. Stacy was Sugar! I was sure of it. But why the ruse, why the elaborate scheme of hiding behind her disguise? What was she after and why didn't I see this sooner? I wondered if Stacy had set me up for Sampson's murder, then come in on her white horse to have me freed. It didn't make sense, though, didn't fit together. Why would Stacy kill Sample? She didn't even know him as far as I knew, but who's to say.

It seemed to me that every question I had, led to other unanswered questions. I had the feeling I was at the tip of the iceberg concerning all this drama in my life lately. Somehow, it was Stacy and not Rochelle who was at the heart of all of my troubles. I just didn't know if Stacy were an ally or an enemy. One thing was for sure, I wouldn't learn a thing in this bed.

I decided to start at Sugarland. I just had a hunch that it was where Stacy rushed off to. It was increasingly difficult for me to trust the two women in my life that I had relied upon before. I had counted on them with life-altering decisions at one point or another; Stacy as my assistant, Rochelle as my wife. Now, both could possibly have stabbed me in the back and laughed as they twisted the knife of betrayal in further.

I had to find the truth before the truth no longer wanted to be found.

Rochelle   27

I was sitting in the parking lot at Sugarland. I had decided to get into Calvin's vehicle while I waited for Jennifer. Calvin drove a dark blue pick-up truck, the kind with the extended cab, which sported a huge interior. We had gotten in the backseat to talk, but he had other plans on his mind.

Calvin cooed in my ear, "Rochelle, I've been thinking about you all day. I can't get your lovely image from running around my head."

He lounged in his backseat while I sat between his long legs, my head resting against his chest. He had my blouse open, had my bra straps lowered and had his hands roaming the exposed flesh of my upper body. He claimed to be giving me a massage but in reality, it appeared he was just copping some serious feels. I didn't object, was juvenile but cute.

I played along, "Damn, Calvin, that feel soooo good. I

didn't realize I was so tense." He placed gentle kisses along the back of my neck while continuing to rub my shoulders. "You have great hands for a young buck," I teased.

"Young buck. I told you these hands could work miracles," he boasted. "But, Ro, I can show you better than I can tell you, ain't no boy living here."

I could see he had taken my jest at his manhood the way I had intended. I felt him rising against my backside. Damn! He was monstrous.

Calvin started nibbling on my left ear, allowed his lips to brush my neck again. My fountain of desires flowed then. I shifted in his lap. Let him see my body's reaction to his machinations. He took my erect nipples between thick pinching fingers, gave me pain then pleasure.

I moaned then stuttered, "C-Calvin...t-that feels so g-g-good." My voice was a soft whisper, could tell he approved.

Calvin continued to grow to massive proportions. I turned around, faced him, gave Calvin eyes of sin, let my intentions be unquestionably known. He took my face into his hands and kissed me deeply. I loved his technique. He explored my mouth with such care, made my tongue dance with his own, wasn't forceful but was very clever in his delivery.

I pulled back, hands resting in his lap. "Damn, Calvin, you got a third leg down there." I grinned, noticed his truck's interior digital clock then. "Let's go inside to wait," I said. "There's more room in there to...ah...stretch out."

Calvin's smile took in his entire face. His eyes got tight. "Sure, Rochelle, whatever you want, but I don't need a whole lot of room to maneuver, I'm pretty flexible with this body of mine."

I breathed. "I just bet you are. Come on please."

"Fine by me, Mrs. Lee," he said.

I got my blouse halfway buttoned up, got out of his truck, and rushed to open the door to the club with Malcolm's keys. Calvin followed as I entered the dark building. I found the lights and motioned for him to follow me to the bar.

"Join me in a drink," I commanded. "I'm buying."

"What's your poison?" Calvin asked. "Brown or white?"

"I like the brown personally," I said, getting the special bottle of Hennessy I had placed behind the counter two days prior. "Pour us a drink while I use the little girl's room and get ready for all of this." I palmed his crotch through his jeans. Damn!

"OK, baby, I got you. Don't take too long, Rochelle. I'll do all the prepping you need." He grinned, undulated his tongue my way.

I damn near floated up the stairs leading to the owner offices and the private restroom in Malcolm's...now...mine! Calvin watched my backside shift this way and that as I did so. I looked back and caught him watching me, twisted even more profoundly for his viewing pleasure.

"It's on," I heard him whisper. "She 'bout to get all this dick up in them guts."

I was just a little worried now. This was more man than I had ever handled, and he was young and apparently going to be aggressive with my Eve. Whatever! I'm the bitch in control here, I told myself as I freshened up. If there's going to be any "turning out " it's going to be me doing the damn turning.

I left my panties on Malcolm's desk, walked back down, determined to tame this "big dicked" young buck. Thoughts of meeting Jennifer all but lost in my desires of this flesh.

Calvin handed me my drink and we did the cheesy intertwine the arms thing and drank from our glasses. He never broke eye contact with me. I shuddered as the warming aspect of the liquid flowed down my throat. He was so damn intense. So was I, was ready to get this party started.

I got in Calvin's personal space, made it ours, kissed him with hunger, allowed his hands to roam my body. His fingers found my Eve as we kissed, found my flower's bulb, massaged it in semi-circles. My heat rose, could feel my tide coming to shore. Calvin continued to manipulate my sex, sensed his approval as he brought his slightly glazed digits to his mouth, savored my taste on his fingers. He gave me his mouth again, shared with me my own flavor, allowed me to relish the taste, made me even more aroused.

Calvin sat on a barstool. I lowered my head, started at his mouth and slowly dropped from nipple, to stomach, to Adam.

I gasped, was still amazed at his length, his incredible size. It looked like a sleeping serpent uncoiled. He was still flaccid, wasn't nearly as erect as he could be. That fact alone gave me pause. Momentarily. I bypassed the length, went straight for the packages underneath. Tongued and kissed his balls with the experience I had gained over time. Calvin moaned, let out a low guttural growl, sounded like a predatory animal.

My tongue explored his southern region then. I found the space between the scrotum and the taboo opening of a man's backside. Licked and sucked on the flesh I found there, got an immediate reaction to my oral deeds. Calvin's fleshy slinky unfolded. He became erect in a way that both frightened and excited me.

I said, "Well, hello there, Mister Happy." I put my two hands around his girth. Barely. I massaged and stroked him then, couldn't believe I actually held a part of a human's anatomy.

He grimaced through his lustful expression. Took my head in a massive hand and guided it to where he believed it would be put to good use. I revealed my understanding by stroking him near the tip of his sex, took over then, parted my lips to accommodate his thick head and gave him wet heat. I began slowly, wanted his lust and desire to build an advance at my pace instead of his own. Eve controlled Adam.

I could only manage a fourth of his length in my mouth, but worked with the inches I could take. I bobbed as I traced his muscled front with the nails of my right hand. He moaned his response.

My lust took hold then, worked my head furiously in vicious jerks and circles. Kept my mouth sloppy, totally saturated with saliva, knew he wouldn't be able to contain himself much longer. I was wrong!

Calvin's whole body seemed to flex and tighten at once. His moans became beastly growls. He stood, raised my head to his by gripping the back of my neck. My mind whirled then. I was somewhat frightened by this powerfully dominate display of Adam controlling Eve. He calmed me at once, as soon as he brought his mouth to mine. Our kiss was wet and sloppy, was nasty, was so damn satisfyingly erotic.

Calvin gave me tight eyes then wrapped one of his huge hands around his Adam, massaged it slow in an up and down motion, eyed my response to his masturbation. My eyes must have given me away, couldn't help but react to what I was witnessing - the largest manifestation of manhood I had ever seen. And it was still growing!

He got all up in my personal space, took my face in his hands, kissed me furiously but tenderly. His dick bobbed north and south bumping against the entrance to my secret garden. As Calvin pulled me into him, it was like I was straddling a horizontal pole of flesh. Damn!

"It's time," he muttered. Calvin picked me up, found a place on the floor just in front of the stage. He pushed my skirt up toward my stomach and opened up my na-na with two thick but skilled fingers. Calvin placed his mouth over my southern one, tongue kissed that one as he had the northern.

I had my legs on his shoulders, feet arched... legs trembling. I couldn't take his sinful tongue. It was much too wicked, too experienced. He explored me, curved his oral appendage to reach my spot, kept running its somewhat rough texture over my silky surface. Whew…wicked tongue twice in the same night!

I screamed, "Calvin…C-Calvin!" I squirmed in his grasp. He had me pinned, couldn't move much. I just had to take what he was serving. I could feel the tingle building, started in my belly, kept rising and rising. He was relentless, wouldn't stop, refused to let up on his dining no matter what I said or how much I pleaded. Calvin devoured me as if I were his last supper.

He raised his head briefly and said, "How sweet it is…how sweet it fucking is."

I tried to give words to what I was feeling. It came out as inaudible gibberish, sounded like I was speaking in tongues, like I had caught the holy-ghost.

Calvin smiled at my orgasmic language, lowered his head once more and fed. He wouldn't surface again until I gushed. I came so hard, so violently. He never ceased his oral manipulations while I was captive and held slave by my uncontrollable orgasms. They were multiple in nature, each bringing me to higher levels of pleasure than the last.

Calvin raised a frothy covered face, he grinned, leveled me with an amoral expression. He moved his body to cover mine, kept my legs resting on his shoulders and placed the tip of his sex at the entrance to my southern heat. He eased himself inside, never going more than a few inches deep. Then he would withdraw to the sounds of wet suctions and my moans. This teasing was even intense, due to his immense size.

I almost lost it. I tried to relax, which was near impossible because of the series of orgasms I had already endured. Calvin's size still worried me but I was determined to conquer my fears. I reached around him, grabbed his tight buttocks and guided him in further.

His stroke was one of heaven and hell, made me weep and smile all at once. He filled me to such capacity that I felt I would never recover from this violation of my sexual insides. Felt like I would long to be filled to such heights for the rest of my life. It would be like a crackhead always searching for the sensation they had from that first hit. I was that far gone.

Calvin was gentle with my Eve initially. Then without warning, he was not. He eased more and more of his length into my womb, went deep with force.

I gasped, shuddered under his erotic dancing thrusts. He was so damn deep! Calvin stood up in me, was proving the nickname he was given - he was laying some serious damn pipe! Pipelayer was correct about his flexibility.

He managed to say, "Gotta get this ass from the back."

I felt him break the connection, felt hollow briefly as a result. Calvin turned me over, pulled me to my knees. I arched my back, let my ass spread with this position. I knew this was what he had longed for the minute he laid lust filled eyes on my motherland ass. This position, doggy style, was his intent all along.

Calvin spread my cheeks as he fed his inches to my sex. He entered. "Oh my God!" I screamed. He wasn't as gentle as before, eased me that meat more forceful this time. I just put my head down and rode the wave gathering in my loins.

The mere facts: Calvin owned more than a foot of dick easily, was young and motivated and was pounding me hard now. He perspired heavily with the thrusting. That length and girth, damn! Calvin was using his flesh-covered ruler to penetrate me with such haste. He gave little regard to my ability to accommodate his size.

It hurt so fucking good. "Baby...shit...f-fuck," I screeched. "Take this...make this pussy yours," I screamed.

Calvin complied, kept thrusting that damn stick of sin all up in my guts. Then without so much as a warning, he pulled out, tried to invade the other opening.

I tensed up, yelled, "No, stop, Calvin!"

He whined, sounded very young then. "Come on, Ro, just let me get the tip in."

"No!" My statement was edged with resolve this time. I turned to look at him, placed my hand on his chest as a restraint, kept him from pressing forward. My breathing was choppy, inhaled and exhaled deeply, tried to get control of my body again.

I say, "Tear this pussy up all you want Calvin. Make it yours, but my ass is off limits, OK?."

He continued to perspire, could feel the heat radiating from his body. His eyes tightened as he gazed at me. I could tell he was one of those men who was not accustomed to hearing the "N" word.

"Ro—," he began.

"No, Calvin, especially with that monster hanging between your legs. You're not busting my ass out and ruining me. It's a struggle just to take what you dishing out to my na-na right now," I teased. "Please respect that or—"

"Fine, Mrs. Lee, I just thought I would take you to the mountain top of orgasms is all. But it's all good, Rochelle."

Calvin fixed me with an unreadable expression, couldn't tell what he was thinking, but I knew he was still aroused. He shrugged then, grabbed my waist, and went deep without warning. I was again immersed in the feeling of being filled to capacity. Damn!

The stroke returned, the dance returned, the pain and pleasure that ruled every nerve ending in my sex returned. They returned with such suddenness, the prior misunderstanding was all but forgotten.

I came too many times to count. They were small but progressing into mega-ton status.

Calvin's hips pumped relentlessly, felt like his Adam was a brush and he was painting a picture in my Eve, a picture of carnal satisfaction. My confidence rose. I began to push back while he stroked forward. My flood-gates opened, coated his sex with sugary goo. I glanced back at him, his head was thrown back, mouth fixed in an O and face fixed with pure ugliness. He enjoyed every moan-bringing thrust being inflicted in my sex.

Foot falls were falling! They fell on deaf ears, could possibly have been due to her barefoot status or more to the fact that there was more than a foot of meat buried deep in my Eve hurting me so fucking good. All I could manage was lurid moans, moans communicating my pleasure, my pain, and my circumstance. My eyes were wide shut, clamped tight, yet my mouth refused to close, waged its war against silence, accompanied Calvin's forceful thrusts, with acoustic delight.

His pumping ceased with such suddenness, my eyes opened on instinct, fell on the sleek gleaming chrome metal, fell on the hand, then the arm, then the body holding the gun just a few feet from my face.

"Finish him, bitch!" she spat.

Deke   28

I **arrived at club Sugarland** under the cover of incomplete darkness. Street lights were on, and the club itself sported a well-lit parking lot, even after the hours of business. Because of city zoning issues, we couldn't stay open past 2 a.m. Monday through Thursday, and that aggravating fact worked in my favor tonight. I could move around pretty much undetected.

The parking lot was barren except for two vehicles, Rochelle's and another. I approached cautiously, decided to pull onto the side road adjacent to our building, didn't want to alert anyone to my presence just yet.

I exited my vehicle and stuffed the gun I had obtained down the front of my jeans, don't know why, but I did. I must have seen someone do that in a movie or something. I had copped a nickel-plated snub nosed .38 revolver, a bit flashy for my tastes, but would more than do the job if I had to use it.

I negotiated the lot with as much stealth as I could, the two vehicles seemed to be abandoned but I couldn't be sure until I checked them. I could clearly see Rochelle's car was empty and dark. The other vehicle, a Ford F150, wasn't as easy to observe due to the dark tinted windows. (front and back)

I moved toward the back of the truck to approach undetected by any occupants within. "Pipelayer" was boldly displayed on the truck's license plate. That alone instantly made my blood boil, 'cause up until that minor discovery, I still held out hope that Rochelle could have been meeting up with one of her girlfriends or something. But with "Pipelayer" on his plates and a big-ass truck no less, there was little doubt as to the gender of its owner.

I crept to the front driver's side door, peered in, didn't see anyone or any movement.

They were inside.

I went around back and let myself in through Sugar's entrance, tip-toed down the hallway past the other dressing rooms, and focused love-weary eyes into the main entertaining area. The image that greeted my limited eyesight was enough to make my soul flee my body.

Rochelle.

Rochelle was being fucked without mercy, was being sexed with little regard to her delicate stature and what's more, she loved every inch of it. I could only stand and stare, was like I was caught in Medusa's gaze, turned to stone, petrified. From my vantage point, I glimpsed my departing sanity's oblivion.

Rochelle was at the front of the stage, near the edge, her

hands gripping that edge. She had her head lowered, back arched, her ass was raised. There were huge hands on both butt cheeks, controlling her, abusing her. He was savagely taking her.

What the savage possessed, didn't even seem real, looked like some fake appendage attached by some perverted surgeon for the purpose of murdering vaginas. He continued to violate her sex…in and out…in and out…in and out. Damn!

My version of hell on Earth was being played out right before me in high definition, in living color. I saw Rochelle's cream start to accumulate around the part of the savage's shaft that wasn't buried deep in her, saw her face, watched the expression of pleasure pain crawl across her visage, saw the ecstasy etched there.

In that moment, I knew—knew I would never—knew I could never, please this sex crazed creature who was sinning before me. I lowered my head briefly, couldn't watch, didn't want to look away. I had loved this woman, my best friend's wife, but loved her just the same.

I heard his guttural moans then, sounded beast-like. He still held his position behind her, had a handful of hair. Pumping so furiously, like he was angry with her Eve, like he was trying to ruin her for any man except himself. Sweat flew from his frame from the sheer exertion of his thrusts. He was straight beastin' the pussy. Rochelle's mouth was frozen in an O. She screamed as he pumped, moaned as he long stroked her, spoke inarticulate gibberish whenever he went too deep.

I leaned in closer, saw his entry point, saw how he

stretched her wide, viewed her lips hugging him tight, saw her grimace and smile while he pumped. He continued to pump like a goddamn madman! Damn!

Rochelle was getting the hell fucked out of her by this horse-dick muthafucka, and by the look on her face, she resided in heaven as a result.

Bitch!

I felt the heat rise then, wasn't flowing from my loins, wasn't sexual heat, was more the fire burning of betrayal.

How dare that bitch!

In that moment, I remembered the extra weight I carried in the front of my pants. I drew it forth, felt it rest easy in my hand, almost was like an extension of my body. It was cold to the touch. Had heard somewhere that revenge was a dish best served cold. This cold contained heat as well. It would be so easy. The two fornicators never even noticed my unwanted presence.

I wiped my water-filled eyes on my sleeves, unclouded my reddened vision, raised an instrument that could orphan babies, pointed to where I believed it would inflict the most destruction.

I stood erect, placed both hands around that bringer of vengeance to steady my aim. I briefly contemplated yelling first, just for the shock value, but wisely decided there would be no warning before my act of retribution.

Footsteps were falling…

I should have heard…

All went black in my world, my last vision was of Rochelle…still   sexing…then   I   was falling…falling…falling.

Sugar   29

I got there just in time to prevent Deke from abducting my rightful destiny. I managed to knock him out and pull him inside my private dressing room. He was not even supposed to be a part of my final plans. We were still enamored with this man.

Deke was special, but he was here. I used a pair of Watts's handcuffs I had taken and cuffed his wrists behind his back, sat him in a chair in the middle of the small enclosure. I used some scarves, tied him to the chair securely. I tied him so he couldn't move a single limb, could only observe and listen.

Deke began to stir. His head moved to and fro, eyes fluttering open, then it happened so suddenly...he was aware.

He gazed at me with a strange expression, asked in a shaken voice, "Sugar?"

"It's me, Deke," I answered. I realized then, Deke had

never seen me without my trademarks. I wore no mask, had no contacts in, and my natural locks flowed down and framed my face.

"What…why…what are you doing here? Why did you hit me on the head and tie me up?"

"Shhhhh, Deke," I said placing two fingers to his lips. "I will tell you all in a minute. Let me check on the lovebirds first."

I left him, slinked down the hallway barefoot, and watched some mighty good fucking going on. Looked like Rochelle was stepping out on Malcolm with Calvin, and his big-dicked ass was giving her more than she could handle. I checked his stroke, noticed his cadence, though he was slamming her viciously, he would be there awhile. I crept back to Deke then.

"Let me go, Sugar…now…S-Sugar," he hissed.

"Why, Deke? What you gonna do…huh…shoot them?" I brandished his gun then held it while I continued to talk. "Listen to me. I didn't go through the depths of hell and back so you could go and fuck up my plans."

"Your plans?" he asked.

"Yes, Deke, I'm going to tell you a story now…short version anyway…then you and you alone will understand."

He remained silent, so I took that to mean he was willing to listen. I began. "There was once a woman-child who was born to a whore. And as whores tend to be, she wasn't exactly the motherly type. She laid with many…many men. As a result, the woman-child never knew the comfort of Daddy, never had the protection of a father, always longed for that connection. A woman-child is not safe in a world of men." My voice lost its sultry tone, sounded high-pitched now, child-like. I spoke from a place I had refused to let surface until this moment. Deke didn't move, didn't try to free himself, he just stared at me, was transfixed by the beginning of my tale. I continued. "The woman-child never learned, never experienced the true way a man is supposed to love a woman, never had the love of a man who protected her virtue. She observed the whore closely, learned the weakness of man, saw how the whore had a measure of control over the opposite sex. She also witnessed the loneliness as well. The loneliness was the catalyst, was what compelled the whore to hate the woman-child, made the whore abuse the child, beat her, allowed the whore to offer the child to men. The whore existed in a world of jealousy and envy for the child. The premature onset of puberty was the woman-child's worst nightmare. She had been coveted by the whore's men before with their perverted thoughts, but now she was truly lusted after. The whore despised the child immensely, likewise the child hated the whore but surprisingly found a small measure of comfort from the perverted men. Eventually, the envious whore sends the child away to live with the whore's sister in another state."

Deke asked simply, "You?" Recognition washed over his face.

I ignored him and continued. "Family life with the sister's brood was ordinary, was somewhat boring for the child. She was born and lived in sin, was a product of that filthy environment. It was a shock to her system but a welcome one. It was briefly a time of forgetfulness, of reinventing oneself; time to heal from too many Uncles and Mama's Friends, time to put the genie back in the bottle. It was an improbable task though, the transformation had already occurred. The woman-child had become a childish woman, had a desirable adult physique at a child's age. As she tried to make new friends, new connections, she recognized the jealousy and envy from her counterparts and the lustful desires from the males she encountered. Still, the child attempted to appear as normal as she could. Until…the one day came, that changed her forever, had released the beast to rule her soul. She was betrayed by a false-friend, was lured to a den of sin and was exposed and raped repeatedly. At the time, the child didn't even associate that act of violence with a violation of her person. It was home, what she was accustomed to. Still she felt the betrayal nonetheless. I felt the betrayal. I was sent away shortly after that incident, got thrown into an institution to…ah…get better. It was more of a Hell than living with the whore. But I survived, Deke. I survived!"

Deke stammered, "A-Ann…little Annie? Y-You look so different, would never have recognized you."

"You used to call me little sis, Deke. You always talked to me, asked me about my day, looked out for me as best you could. I always had a huge crush on you back then."

Deke looked as if he were seeing a ghost. "I heard about what happened to you that day. I wished I were there, Annie, wished I could have spared you that hurt."

"I believe you, Deke. You were always good to your Lil' Annie as you called me. But Anastacia died that day and was reborn into what stands before you now." I walked to Deke, leaned in closer, showed him my resolve, put my hand inside the front of his pants, held him, felt the electricity of his manhood come to life in my grasp. Then I kissed him with the passion of 10 years of imprisonment. Kissed him rough, tenderly, kissed him with love I felt for him, let all I had enter that kiss, that connection. When finished, Deke simply stared, had no words, his expression spoke volumes, though. I said, "It ends tonight, Deke. I have always loved you. Now you and you alone know the truth."

"Annie…wait! Don't do this!"

"Do what, Deke? Don't free myself from this pain? Remember your Lil Annie. Forget all about Sugar, OK?. That would be best for you." I grinned , kissed the head of his Adam, sucked the crown for a few seconds, left him with that sinful memory. Then I walked out and left the only male I ever respected to his own private thoughts.

$ $ $

I came upon the sinning as silent as a whisper, gun still in hand, stood before the fornicators and became the voyeur for a few moments. I glimpsed, then heard Rochelle's emphatic refusal for anal play with Calvin's massive member. Then I remembered. "Finish him, bitch!" I yelled.

Time stopped, stood stagnant, was very still. Rochelle raised her head slowly, was difficult with all that meat buried deep. I gave her the smile of the insane, held the chrome I carried boldly. She knew. She understood. She saw her end in my eyes. I stood confident before her, allowed her fate to quickly sink in. My smile widened even further as I saw recognition creep across Rochelle's visage.

I repeated, "Finish him, bitch!"

Calvin's eyes bulged, fixated on the chrome I brandished. I could feel his fear, his measure of familiarity with insane women aiming bastard makers toward his person. "Relax, Pipelayer," I said with my sultry tone returning. "Trust me, you need to calm down a bit."

He stuttered, "M-m-miss, t-this ain't what it look like."

"Miss? Calvin it's me Sugar. We just met a few days ago, and, damn, you done gone and forgotten about little ole me already."

It took his mind some time to work, what with all that blood flow going to his southern region, but soon he understood I was who I claimed to be. "Sorry, didn't recognize you without the mask and stuff."

I eased closer as we spoke, did so like the cobra inches closer before striking its prey. "Well, Mister Pipelayer, how 'bout you finish the little show you and the lovely and adulterous Miss Rochelle were putting on before I so rudely interrupted."

Rochelle managed, "S-Stacy, I…"

"Shut up, bitch! Now, Calvin, commence to fucking her precious tight ass right now," I commanded.

"B-b-but, Sugar…"

I passed by the nearly empty bottle of Hennessy, committed the remaining level to memory, knew my time was about to end shortly from this satisfying amusement.

Rochelle was a creature of habit. She pretty much kept

her scandalous life consistent. Never really wavered from her personal deviations, same type of men to play with, same places to shop at, same old boring-ass Hen-N-Coke to drink. I knew she would try one of the male dancers, just waited to see which one, knew she would drink her predictable Hennessy with a hint of coke. Just waited for the right time then I jumped. Glad she accepted the little gift Watts had given her courtesy of Sugar.

Stupid bitch!

"Go on, Calvin. Lay some more of that big-ass pipe." He went limp with the gun aimed at his chest, still an impressive site though. I went around the now-dislodging couple, Rochelle still on all fours, Calvin behind her on his knees, dick hanging between Rochelle's lovely buttocks.

I got behind Calvin, gun aimed at Rochelle's backside, sucked on his earlobe; licked the nape of his neck. Calvin's reaction to my manipulations pleased me. I found his dick with my free hand, stroked him slow along with his balls, felt and saw the pipe grow again, got rigid, got "longer-er." I held him for a moment, relished his member's weight and size, aimed him for her juicy backside, aimed for the taboo hole. "Fill her," I said. Calvin needed no more motivation for my request. He pushed and pushed. Rochelle screamed as if she were being ripped open…wide. I smiled, admired her lovely backside that rivaled my own. "Take that ass, Calvin. Take it!" If I were male and possessed an Adam, I would want to plunge it deep as well. Rochelle was too tight, too dry, so I spit on his member, spit repeatedly so he could work it in. I got up, walked around them, faced Rochelle, reveled in the intense pain I knew that massive dick was inflicting.

The joy I felt was immeasurable. Rochelle, gun to her face, had no other recourse but to just take it. Her arms and hands were flexed out in front of her torso, head was down, mouth opened in a perpetual scream. "Like that, bitch?" I teased. Then without warning the toxin took effect on Mister Pipelayer. Calvin fell over on his back, tried to clutch his chest. I knew the toxin I used wouldn't allow him to do so.

"Shhh…S-Sugar…what," he croaked.

"Sorry, babe. I guess you got caught in the wrong place, in the wrong pussy. You're just an unfortunate casualty of war I'm afraid. That neurotoxin I used, works faster on your nervous system then your heart when you physically exert yourself. And, Calvin, you've been fucking the shit out of Miss Rochelle here for the better part of 30 minutes or so. I really don't think your heart can take much more."

His eyes bulged, face contorted to express the pain I knew he must feel. Heart attacks are brutal, I'm told. Then, just like that, his fight was over. I grabbed his manhood, studied its length again. Damn, what a shame. I shook my head. I was going to give him some Sugar, too. Then my smile returned. I laughed, was more of a cackle, sounded witch-like, turned to Rochelle who was lying on her stomach unable to move. She still struggled from the drug and the reaming she just received from that monstrous dick.

She whimpered.

I teased, "Rochelle, Rochelle. Up and at 'em, bitch!" I rolled her over to face me, brought my mouth inches from hers, then spit in her goddamn face.

"S-Stacy, please, I don't know what this is all about." She whispered, but her words echoed in my ears.

I said, "You don't know, Rochelle. Really! Take a real good look at me, Ro. Look past the hair, the body, the confidence standing before you."

Rochelle strained to scrutinize my image.

I screamed, "Chunky A, bitch. That was what you used to call me behind my back...Chunky A."

Her eyes went wide. "An-Anastacia," she breathed.

"Yes, Ro. I finally came back to get even with all you muthafuckas who helped to murder my childhood, to take away my reclaimed innocence. Yeah, bitch, take it all in. I did this to you. You are on the verge of death's door because of me, and I must say you have more than provided me with some much-needed amusement."

My saliva slithered down the left side of her face. I raised her head so our gazes were locked to one another. Then I saw her small mind working. "You're the one who helped Jennifer," she accused.

"Helped? Bitch, I orchestrated the whole fucking thing. It was me who manipulated Watts to manipulate your dumb ass. Malcolm...gay." I cackled. "Your ignorant ass believed that skirt-chasing muthafucka was sword fighting. No, Rochelle, it was all a lie. You brought down your precious family on a lie and on the end of Jennifer's wicked and talented tongue."

"Bitch!" she spat, somewhat slurred.

"Remember, Ro, it was you all those years ago that coaxed my naïve ass into going to Black's that day. 'Come on, Ann,' you said. 'You can dance in a bathing suit and make some money.'" I smacked the bitch's left cheek hard then. "You let them drug me, allowed Sampson to violate my reclaimed innocence with that big-ass dick of his. I was never the same after that, Ro. They raped me for hours after you left with Malcolm. They raped and dropped me off in front of my home, hurt and raw." If this were a movie, a film or such, I would have had tears streaming from my eyes, flowing down my face in this moment. But there were no tears left to shed. They had been spent years prior. There was only Sugar—Sugar who was the embodiment of vengeance, of cold-blooded truth.

Rochelle tried to speak. Her words became as inaudible now as when she was getting banged by Calvin and that pipe. The toxin had paralyzed her, made speech almost impossible.

I straddled her, took my tongue and licked her navel, went north after, found her full lips, kissed her roughly and bit her bottom lip till I probably drew blood. She couldn't move, was frozen, frozen but aware. I knew she physically felt every touch, every little sensation her skin relayed to her brain. She was robbed of her movement but not her sense of feeling.

I stood, took my panties off, stepped out of my skirt. Then I brought my Sugar, my Eve, to Rochelle's shocked face. Her eyes spoke that she knew it was over, that Sugar had prevailed. Told me she was afraid to die, to expire this way, at this time. I looked down on her, gave her the face of the Joker, lowered my southern lips to her northern lips. This would be my final dance at club Sugarland.

I swayed, hips rolling, body contorting, smothered her

face with ass and twat, with essence of Sugar…dammit! Made her taste me, inhale me. I knew I had started to drip on her lips. I had held his cum in me for hours, now it began to seep, had marinated well in my heat. I continued to dance, forced more onto her lips, then passed them, got to her mouth. "Yes, bitch, that's it. Taste your husband's nut. You've had it before, just not mixed with Sugar."

Rochelle's eyes went wide. "You know Ro, I'm glad you interrupted us that night in DC. You saved your husband's life that night and didn't even realize it. I wasn't just fucking Malcolm when you stormed in on us. I was going to kill him that night. Let you live out your miserable days without the love of your life. That was my plan then. But this turned out to be so much sweeter…don't you think?"

I churned my hips more forceful, started to really ride her face.

"I paid him a visit when they let him out—oh yeah, you did hear Malcolm is free, didn't you? They found the real killer it would seem." I grinded even harder in her face, cut off her air supply, felt the beginning stages of an orgasm forming. I imagined her arms flailing about, her legs extended and kicking, had to fantasize these reactions because I understood the neurotoxin eliminated these anticipated responses to my suffocation of Rochelle. Still, this deadly pussy of mine was no imagination. I moved my sex back and forth over her face, particularly her mouth, felt so damn good, I came hard as she died beneath me. Yes, the last thing Rochelle saw was my muff in her face. The last thing she smelled was Sugar and her last taste was of this Eve and nectar from her husband's Adam.

I laughed and laughed and laughed. "Now it's done, bitch!"

I got off of Rochelle, stared at her lifeless form. A tiny speckle of remorse entered my hate-filled frame. She had been similar to us in many ways, was a perfect rival in that respect. If she had not been one of the perpetrators of my insanity, we might have been friends even lovers, but that was not to be our fate and she had just met hers compliments of Sugar!

After putting my panties and skirt back on, I surveyed the scene intently. Calvin was not part of my plan. He needed to be dealt with. I had to dispose of his considerable bulk somehow, and I could tell he would be too much for me to lift. I would need some aide.

I went to Deke. He still remained seated in the middle of my dressing room, lost in his thoughts I would imagine. He still had not even tried to break free or loosen his bonds.

Deke raised a solemn face as I approached. "Back to finish me off now, Sugar?" he asked.

I stood before him, was silent for a few long standing moments, let my lack of an answer make him question who I really was. That was the Sugar in me, she who was akin to Lilith, she who proclaimed that it was Eve who ruled Adam, who looked down her nose on males as only playthings and useful tools for one to manipulate. But it was I who answered. "No, Deke, I could never do that. I cared about you deeply once in another life. Besides, I wouldn't deprive the world of such a talented lover." I grinned the grin of a predator. "It's just too bad you got stuck on Rochelle and we never picked back up where we left off. But it is what it is."

He shifted, appeared nervous, saw him trying to figure out my angle with this idle chatter. "I didn't hear any gunshots," he inquired. "Is Rochelle…?"

"Dead," I answered matter-of-factly. "It's over, and now I need your help. I'll make it easier on your conscience, though." I raised Deke's gun, pointed it his way. "I'm going to untie you now, Deke. Please don't make me kill you. Believe me, it's the last thing I want, but I will if you push me."

"What do you want, S-Sugar?" he said, venom dripping with the simple uttering of my name.

"Just a little man power, Deke…but first."

I came upon Deke's front, untied the scarves that pinned his legs and torso. His pants were still open in the front from before. I lowered my head, gave him heat, placed my hands behind my back to mimic his current posture. No hands! Used my northern orifice to give him pleasure, gave him slow and deliberate satisfaction, was all mouth. Deke's head fell backward. He moaned his delight, said my name. I no longer existed as Annie to him anymore, was only Sugar now. He understood, let me gift him with this. Then he came violently, filled my mouth with his desire. I swallowed and smiled, savored his taste, committed it to memory. Kissed his Adam, then I returned it to the confines of his pants. I uncuffed Deke, still held the pistol but didn't aim it his way. I waited for Deke to decide.

We walked out together.

Deke   30

Sugar let me live. She left me in a state of shock, but I still was left breathing, which is more than I can say for Rochelle. My eyes watered just thinking about the scene Sugar had led me to, Rochelle, still naked, lying on her back, eyes open, seeing nothing. Couldn't help but sob uncontrollably at that sight. She didn't move. There was no rise and fall of her chest, just a beautiful shell with no soul present.

The savage that had been ravishing her was on his back, just off to the right. He was motionless as well, pants were bunched around his ankles, his huge privates exposed and proudly displayed. It looked to me that his passing was terribly painful. His final expression was horrid, locked on his face. I walked toward them and vomited. The stench that abused my nose facilitated that response. The fucking savage had soiled himself, and it began to reek. Bastard!

I turned and gazed at Sugar then saw her reaction to the

imagery she had a hand in bringing about. Sugar was void of emotion, looked at the bodies as nonchalant as if she were watching television. I took that all in, processed her actions after her crimes. I realized then that the Lil' Annie I knew way back when was gone forever. There was only Sugar now. There was only revenge, was no love present.

I asked, "How...how did you do it?"

"Well, Deke," she said. "After my stint inside the Institution, I tried my hand at college life. I was a biology major at Clark in Atlanta, had an internship with Johnson's Biomedical Laboratories. They were the leading force behind some of the world's most potent and powerful neurotoxin discoveries. Funny thing about this one, though. It bonds with alcohol of any kind. Once bonded, it becomes virtually odorless and tasteless. And, Deke, once it is introduced into the blood stream, it begins to work almost immediately on the nervous system, but its effects are slow to manifest themselves until it is too late. Works a lot faster if the heart is beating rapidly from some type of physical exertion like...ah...fucking. Sugar cackled loudly. Thought I was Dorothy in the Land of Oz for a moment. "That's why Pipelayer lying over there expired first. He was straight beastin' Rochelle's kitty-cat, so it worked on him a lot quicker."

I surveyed Rochelle's frame, eyes falling on her lovely but expressionless face. Then it occurred to me. Why didn't Rochelle wear the same horrid expression on her face as the savage had on his?

"You finished her off, didn't you, Sugar?" My question fell on deaf ears.

She said, "Deke, just do what I ask of you, please. The less you know, the better. But since you asked, yes, I gave that bitch some of this pussy before she departed."

I could well imagine what that death must have been like for an alpha female like Rochelle. I could tell Sugar had a measure of calmness and relief after taking Rochelle out, almost as if her purpose had been served.

I could see her more clearly now, glimpsed that part of her that was real. Sugar was the creation of Anastacia, forged from a troubled soul that was haunted by her past. After that realization, she no longer held the sexual fantasy that once clouded my mind, was more than an instrument of desire for me. I must confess, I once viewed her in two-dimensional terms, like she was a character on television, someone to gawk at, to appreciate in only sexual terms. Sugar was human, though, had emotions, was fractured. She had been broken at her core.

I pitied her!

After my involvement in her crimes after the fact, she tied and handcuffed me again, left me upstairs in the VIP section this time, so I could clearly be seen when someone entered the main room.

Before she left me in solitude, she said, "You always treated me with respect, Deke. That's why you still got your life. But think on this. You can choose to tell the police everything you know when they arrive, but Sugar is gone, was really never here, just a fantasy. There is no one linking me to anything except you, and you will never know when Sugar will return."

I understood her statement loud and clear. There was

really little need for her threat. I would keep the truth about Sugar for as long as I lived. She kissed me gently one last time, got up and strutted out of my life like the sexual vixen she was. But just before, she turned around and said, "Oh, and, Deke…you're welcome!" Then she was gone.

I pondered her last statement for some time. Didn't understand what she meant by it. She was obviously implying something important. I guess I should have thanked her more profusely for allowing me to live.

As I sat there contemplating the night's turn of events, chaos emerged through the club's doors.

Malcolm 31

I arrived to what looked to be normalcy at club Sugarland. At least it appeared that way outside in the parking lot. Everything appeared to be status quo aside from my wife's car sitting alone in the lot. Rochelle was apparently here, didn't see any sign of Stacy's vehicle. I had this eerie feeling emanating from my gut. Didn't like what it could possibly mean—like my intuition was telling me to beware.

I entered Sugarland with much trepidation. It was dimly lit, couldn't see much. The atmosphere was an ear-splitting quiet. The type of silence that was unnatural. I walked in further, saw my wife lying on the floor, heard sobs wafting down from the VIP section.

"Rochelle!" I yelled. Ran to her, laid her head in my lap, ran my fingers through her disheveled hair. Was strangely familiar, this scene was. But this was my wife, dammit! She wasn't moving, wasn't breathing. Rochelle was dead. My mind raced. How? Why? What? All were queries I had no answers to. So I cried, cried for my twin boys, for my lovely wife who understood me better than anyone. I cried because our life together was over. Though she was about to leave me, I still loved her, figured we would eventually work things out the way we always had. That was impossible now. There would be no reconciliation, no make-up lovemaking. Someone had snuffed out the mother of my children. Dammit!

I raised my head. Eyesight fell on someone sitting in a chair at the top of the stairs. That was where the sobs were coming from. It was Deke! He hadn't even noticed my presence yet, was still grieving over my wife, I would guess. I was still trying to wrap my mind around this macabre scene, trying to figure out the unsolvable at this point.

I laid Rochelle's head back on the floor, got up, went to the bar, poured myself a drink.

Needed that.

Took the alcohol with one gulp, savored the burn going down. Thought it would help me wake from my mental fog.

"Malcolm," Deke called my name then.

I sat on a barstool, poured myself another drink.

"Malcolm…help me…Ro is dead, man. I-I don't know what the fuck is going on. Someone hit me on the back of the head, knocked me out, then tied me up."

I drained another drink, raised my head Deke's way then lowered it. My eyes fell on a shiny piece of metal on the bar as I hefted the liquor bottle again.

Deke continued to shout. "Malcolm…Malcolm!"

"I'm coming, Deke," my voice barely above a whisper. I moved as if in quicksand. Stood. I walked slowly, very deliberate in my stride. I had a purpose to my stagnant gait. My hands were not empty. I took the stairs leading to Deke, one at a time. My hands were not empty.

As I reached the top of the stairway, I raised my left hand, took a swig from the bottle of tequila I held. I looked Deke dead in his eyes the way he once did to me, raised my right hand, the one holding the chrome-plated gun. *I'm fucking Rochelle,* continued to ring in my ears, they were the last words Deke spoke to me before now.

He said, "M-m-malcolm, what are you doing. Man, I didn't do that to Ro."

I'm fucking Rochelle...

"Malcolm, please man. I didn't do this. I loved her, too, dammit! Oh God..."

Fucking Rochelle...

"No, Malcolm!"

I didn't say a word, was just me and the gun. We were one, alone in this nightmare. I pointed and squeezed ever so gently, squeezed repeatedly.

Sugar 32

"Harder, Jake...fuck me harder, dammit!" I squealed like a piglet, moaned as if I was getting the best Adam I had ever had.

It worked.

I looked around the interior of the work van Dr. Jacob Lawson had managed to secure for this little off-the-clock rendezvous. I was surprised he had been able to get away from his wife at such an hour, but here he was, banging my Eve with all he had to offer, which wasn't much. Honestly, his stroke wasn't that bad, was actually pleasing to me. He had the van rocking, had the cases of empty vials clinking together as he continued to pump me with all he was worth. We were parked in the empty parking lot of his company, off to the side, kind of hidden from view. It was private.

I was on all fours with the fool behind me. Figured he would put his hard hat on and work me over good in this position.

I was right.

He yelled, "I-I-I'm coming, Sugar!"

Then he fell away just as sudden as his release. I turned, glanced back at him, and smiled. "Glad you got one final nut, Jake," I said. There was no answer from the good doctor. His heart had stopped. He never knew what hit him, I bet.

I pulled my skirt back down, took the condom off his Adam, dragged him to the driver's seat. I left his pants around his ankles, placed his boxers so they rested just above his knees. I then squeezed the condom, dripping his semen all over his softening manhood and on his right hand. Left him in that state, wiped out all existence of Sugar ever being in that van. Then I fled.

I was through with Durham for now, had other things to attend to. Watts had used her considerable contacts to give me the information I needed to finish this. I missed her already. I placed my truck on highway 85 going north, wouldn't stop till I reached Virginia.

I whispered, "Goodbye, Deke." I did so before I crossed the state line.

I drove most of the way with a wicked grin plastered on my face.

Deke   33

I opened my eyes to the light. It was a new day. The sun shined brightly through the partially opened blinds in my house. It would be my last day here. I was glad to be alive, wanted to start off fresh, make a better life for myself. I sure had been through a hell of a lot lately.

Malcolm had asked me to go back to D.C. with him. To help out with my nephews, was what he had said, but I knew he just wanted to get me out of Durham. Black was getting out in a couple of days. We both knew what that meant. I was definitely down with getting the hell out of Dodge. Distant cousins or no, I knew he would never forgive, wasn't in his insane nature or his cold heart. Probably was for the best that I had made an enemy such as him. Made leaving the Bull City that much easier. Besides, Malcolm and the boys were family.

I must say, when Mal had that gun pointed my way, I thought I was a dead man. I deserved no less. I had said a final silent prayer and closed my eyes, heard the gunshots firing but never felt the heat. Malcolm shot the lights out of the neon sign on the wall behind me. Simply said he forgave me. We had a long heart-to-heart talk while we waited for the police to arrive.

It turned out the cops knew a lot more than we did. They still took us downtown for questioning and not for booking.

Whew!

Detective Davis, the principle investigator on Malcolm's murder case, told us pretty much what had transpired leading up to that night's events. He said, "Your friend Sampson and his partner Jennifer Watts were pretty much dirty-ass cops, and what's more they apparently were lovers." Davis continued, "It would appear Officer Watts found out that Officer Sampson had some sort of obsession with Mrs. Rochelle Lee. She then befriended Mrs. Lee and became her subsequent lover."

I was floored. Rochelle had been fucking Sample's girl, and none of us knew it. Malcolm just sat there and listened, didn't ask any questions, just remained silent. Davis said, "They got together and came up with a scheme to get rid of you Mr. Lee and Sampson while also obtaining control of your considerable assets."

"So this was all about money...fucking greed!"

"It would appear so, Mr. Plummer. They planned it all out to the slightest minute detail. This was the best frame job this department has ever come across. It was fucking brilliant." Davis was awestruck by the bitches' cunning it seemed.

I asked, "How did you guys finally figure all this out?"

"Well...to tell the truth, we didn't. It seems Officer Watts developed a conscience along with her insane ways. She couldn't live with what she had done. Wrote a full confession detailing every illicit act she and Mrs. Lee committed. She took herself out with a poisoned cocktail, but not before knocking you out and taking out her partner in crime. Why were you and Mrs. Lee at the club again?" he asked.

"Told you...I was there doing some paperwork. I never even saw Rochelle or Officer Watts for that matter. All I know is someone cold-cocked me on the back of the head, and when I came to, I had been tied and handcuffed. That's when I first laid eyes on Rochelle's lifeless body, then Malcolm showed up and freed me."

"And the gunshots..."

I shook my head. "I don't know what to tell you, Detective Davis."

"Uh-huh," Davis muttered. He didn't seem too convinced with my version of events, but every word I spoke could not be disproved by the evidence so he just dropped it. For now. "Well, be that as it may, we seem to be done here. The both of you are extremely lucky to be alive." He focused on Malcolm then. "And the Department regrets any inconvenience we may have caused you, Mr. Lee. Also I am personally sorry for your loss." Davis reached out his hand to shake ours. I just stared at it. Malcolm did likewise.

Malcolm said, "My attorney will be in touch, Mr. Davis."

We exited the police department both with heavy hearts but glad to be leaving and not staying.

Malcolm phoned me the next day, asked me a multitude of questions. I knew he would. Had already mentally prepared myself for the onslaught. I gave him the same story I had relayed to the cops. He asked me where Sugar was. She hadn't been seen lately, had apparently vanished. The same could be said about his former secretary from D.C. who had been responsible for his freedom from the slammer. Mal was convinced she was Sugar. I just let him come up with his own conclusions. I chose to remember Lil' Annie as she was before the incident. She was already flawed when I met her, but still held a certain kind of innocence about her,. Now there was only Sugar, an instrument for vengeance, a sexual predator.

The next day, we headed for the District early that morning. As we drove down 85 headed north, I couldn't help but hope that someday Sugar would find peace in this world. I hoped she could one day leave the past in the past and find a sense of freedom.

I also thought about Black trying to find me and exact his own type of revenge. Oh well…good luck finding this brotha in Chocolate City.

I glanced at Malcolm, turned, and looked at my nephews in the backseat, saw Rochelle's image in their own faces. I would help to insure her offspring never forgot the type of mother she was. I had accepted her for who she was. I believed Malcolm had as well. Rochelle was complex to say the least. She manipulated the both of us. We both still had love for her, though.

My mind wandered back to the conversation we had with Detective Davis, the things he shared with us about the lengths Rochelle and Watts had gone through to frame Malcolm were just sick: from obtaining his sperm on the sneak tip, to using a dildo on Sampson while he was dead to simulate anal sex, to pouring Mal's semen in Sample's anus. Rochelle was not the woman I believed her to be, but I couldn't help the way I felt. I'm sure Malcolm felt somewhat the same way I did.

It's never good to fall for wicked women.

Black   34

I sat alone in my cell, shook my head as I read the morning paper, was in a state of absolute shock and denial. It seems that Durham added another homicide to its infamous list. This time it was my cousin, my fucking li'l sister... Rochelle. I tried to ignore the lone tear struggling on its journey down my face as I read. I fumed while sitting there feeling helpless. They weren't revealing too much, which was typical of the DPD in these instances, but what the article did have to report was a bit scandalous in nature.

Apparently Rochelle had partnered up with Sample's crooked-ass sidekick, and the two were reported to have some type of involvement in his murder. The paper also hinted at them possibly planting evidence to frame Rochelle's husband, Malcolm, for the crime. I smiled at that. I really didn't know my little sis had it in her. But my smile quickly faded as the reality of Rochelle's fire being snuffed out for good began to sink in.

The paper named Jennifer Watts as the prime suspect in Rochelle's murder. Said that the bitch took her own life after killing Rochelle, also said Deacon Plummer and Malcolm Lee were at the scene of the crime and were taken in for questioning but were released shortly after.

I stood, paced my six by nine, walked back and forth. Those muthafuckas knew something, had to have something to do with this shit. I rushed the bars of the cell with the force of a caged animal, which I was. Yelled for the guard on duty.

"Yeah…what do you want, Black?" Detention Officer James Turner, a menacing mountain of a man and one of the foulest guards on the floor said.

"I need to talk with Chi-town man. Is he on duty now, Turner?" James Turner eyeballed me up and down, could tell he held a certain amount of disgust for my person, like he hated to share the same air I breathed. Yet the nigga didn't mind taking the green that I lined his pockets with for the purpose of extra privileges up in this liquor house.

Sammy Santiago, who was known as Chi-town for obvious reasons, was the man to go to for any issues you had under the roof of this jailhouse. He made things happen.

"Yeah…he's here, Black. What tha fuck do you want or need now?"

I eyeballed him. "I need to make a call, man."

"You don't need Chi for that, nigga. You know the procedures for making calls," Turner growled.

"No, Negro, I need to make…a call," emphasizing the last word so he would understand my meaning. Turner nodded then turned to get the leader of the two. He was just the muscle around this place, but Chi-town was the brains and the man in charge. If you had enough green, you could get whatever you wanted or needed just like you were on the outside. Now I need a disposable phone to make some untapped calls.

Chi-town appeared minutes later. He was a big Latino, could pass for a light-skinned brotha if he chose to, was maybe just a couple of inches short of my 6'8 frame. Santiago always had a smile plastered on a face that wasn't quite symmetrical, eyes were too close together, nose was long an angular. He was as insane as people claimed me to be, was just as sadistic. (if not more). Here was a stone-cold killer who had a badge. He was smart, though, and business minded, which I liked.

"What's up, Black," he said. "Damn, bro, you getting out in the morning and you want to make a PAID call now. It must be important."

"That's my business Chi," I countered.

"Uh-huh…importance might drive the price up a bit, big boy," he teased. "So what's so damn important that can't wait until morning?"

I shoved the newspaper in his face. "My cousin…and little punk-ass Deacon Plummer for one."

Santiago nodded. He knew what my relationship had been with Rochelle. Hell, everyone did. She visited me on the regular and was kind of a fixture around the jailhouse. "OK, Black, we all feel bad about Ro, but she got herself caught up in some serious shit. Murder…planting evidence…and well, being a little free with that pretty ass of hers."

"Watch your damn mouth, Chi," I threatened. "Respect my little sis or…"

"Or what, nigga," he challenged. "Don't forget who the fuck I am in here, muthafucka. You reside in my house. You still got some hours left before we have to cut you loose, so you show the proper respect…nigga!"

Turner approached my cell then, guess he had overheard our exchange. The look he gave me promised a swift death if I continued down this path. I returned that look with a promise of my own. I said, "No disrespect meant, Chi. I just need to make some calls and fast. Need to get my people to do some digging before Deke skips town."

"You wouldn't be calling in a hit while you in my lock-up on one of my cell phones, now would you, Black?"

"Naw, man, I just want to talk to Deke. Just talk." I couldn't even hide the lie from my voice, but I knew Santiago didn't care. He was just probing for an angle to drive the cost of the phone up. It mattered little to me at this point.

"OK, Black, give me 'til tonight. I got a fresh shipment of throw-away coming in."

"Tonight!"

"Yeah tonight, nigga…you going somewhere or something?" He left me then.

Turner lingered at the door for a few seconds. He was silently challenging me. I seethed but got my temper in check, sat back down on my bunk. Turner smiled at my backing down, then left. I would just have to wait for a few things, I told myself as I watched him leave. But I would not have to stop thinking of ways to torture that back-stabbing-ass Deke, once I got my hands on him, and now as I considered Turner's boldness toward me, Deke just might have some company.

It was late that night when the door to my cell opened. I was asleep, but barely. One always slept lightly in lock-up. I opened my eyes to two hulking shadows. It was dark, but they were clothed in black or at the very least dark clothing. I couldn't make out their faces but by their sizes, I determined they must be Tuner and Santiago.

"Did you bring it, Chi-town?" I asked.

The cell door closed behind them, they both approached me slowly. "Money..." The smaller of the two demanded. "Three bills, Black."

I nodded, stood, turned and lifted the front of the mattress off my bunk to get at the stash I kept there. I had my back to them very briefly as I counted. That was how I was caught unaware.

I felt the blow come first at the back of my left knee, made that leg buckle, but before losing my balance completely, I felt the oh-too-familiar hardness of a police-issue nightstick at my throat. It was placed there with such force, I figured it had to have crushed my windpipe. The pressure kept increasing, continued cutting off my air supply. They had me in a standard choke hold that was usually reserved for the brothas. I figured it was Turner who had me subdued and near death in this position. Only his near seven feet could yank my 6'8 frame from the floor the way I had been.

My feet were lifted by the other assassin. I realized then that there would be no freedom for Blackwell Barnes come the morning, no revenge on Deke, no retribution for Rochelle, no nothing. I had been a menace to the Earth the day I was born, reveled in that, got a hard on at times because of the fear and pain I inflicted on the weak and the addicted. but now It was finally my goddamn turn!

I started to lose consciousness as air fled my body, my eyes bulged, felt like they were just about to pop out of their sockets. My ending was almost here, but before I expired, Santiago dropped my feet, came close to my face, smug grin on his face. He whispered," Sugar says hello, bitch!"

Epilogue

Steven Hawkins, captain of the "Freespirit," a quaint little charter fishing boat, continued to eyeball his lone passenger. He grinned sheepishly as he thought about how he had bedded this sexy young vixen just a few hours prior. He had encountered her at his favorite late-night bar overlooking the docks where his boat was housed. He quickly turned on the charm, enticed her to have some adult fun before someone else cast their bait her way. She had agreed.

She had asked him to take her out on the water, once she learned he was captain of his own vessel. She claimed to want to try some night fishing, but he figured the little sex kitten wanted to sex on the sea. He eagerly complied with her request, took her and her overly abundant luggage out on his boat.

Hawkins being a married man, had few chances for these illicit affairs, and he wanted to enjoy this lovely creature to the fullest. He would deal with the consequences and his wife in the morning.

"Hey, Steve," the vixen cooed. "It's so dark out here. I wonder...did you tell anybody we were going out?"

He answered, "Not yet, babe, was just about to radio our position in a moment. 'Bout ready to drop anchor...come 'ere, let me show you how to operate it." Captain Hawkins loved showing off his boat. It gave him a sense of pride when he could talk about his baby to others.

The vixen grinned widely, took her top off then, strutted closer to the captain. His eyes were fixated on two perfect breasts, nipples standing at attention due to the cool breeze coming from the sea. Captain Hawkins never noticed the iron weight in her hand before it connected with his skull. Steve Hawkins' world went as black as the ocean at night.

"That's all I needed to know, baby," Sugar said.

She began to toss what she carried in those luggage bags over the side of the boat, had already spotted some dorsal fins breaking the water just minutes before, knew they fed nightly. Once she dumped her cargo, she pushed the good captain over the side, hoping the sharks would take care of him as well. Then she took the inflatable raft, placed it along with her remaining luggage in the water, got in and began to paddle. It was a long way to shore, and she knew she would have to swim part of the way.

She relaxed as she paddled. It was peaceful out there in the water along with the other predators. She had time to think, had time to plot.

One name still remained on her list!

Acknowledgements

First I would like to give all the glory to his Holiness, without whom none of this would be possible.

Well let me say this was a journey. A long one in the making. There are so many people who have touched my life in such profound way as to give me hope and belief; it would take a book just to name them. I will attempt to name a few and if I have forgotten anyone, please be patient with me, it's just the first of many books to come. I'll get you in one of them.

Ok here we go: First thanks to Tasha Johnson, wouldn't be a Sugarland without you! We did it,babe! I'd like to thank my children: Kaylin, Jalen and Harper, My parents: Oleta Woyee, Grady L. Sanders, Elijah Woyee, Barbara Sanders. The Fam': Kimberly Sanders-Johnson, Kevin Pickett, TanNeisha Sanders and the cuzo's: Tonya Adams, Lisa Adams, LaTasha Sanders, James Sanders, Nikkie Sanders, Towanda Rhodes.Uncle Larry Sanders, Aunt Grace Adams, Aunt Marion Sanders the entire

Sanders/Pickett/Rhodes Family. The other Fam: Patrick Plummer, Cheryl and Cliff Vincent, Clint Vincent and Charity, Carinto Vareene, Mrs.Madeline Plummer, Mr.Willie Plummer, Princess and Quincy Pedew, LaShea and Tarez Thorbs, Gwen and Mike, Debbie, Bojangles. To Lisa Wilson-Sullivan, thanks for being a great friend for almost all of my life. Big ups to Rahee Sullivan…you are next! Thank you to Edna Pauline for helping in any and every way you could. Tracy and Gina giving you thanks (Chi-town)! Patrice Johnson and the boys, The Friends: John and Pauline Fitzpatrick, Barb and Sharlene thank you for everything!, Kesia Tucker, Carlton Hopkins, Tony Pratt, Leon Justice, Derrick Brown, Germaine Jones, Bobby and Sherai Jones, Gwyn Davis, Tonya "T-Bell" Ferrell, Kevin Mosely, David Wiggins and thanks to the host of friends who have escorted me on my journey through life. A special thanks to Felicia Kersey Angus for the Dirty H2O! It's a hit! Once again, thank you all…

A Bonus Chapter from the Upcoming

Novel:

Sugar-free

Ann   1

It had been 3 months since I left Durham in my rearview mirror. I had landed in a small town in Virginia, was getting use to this laid back lifestyle for awhile. I had found work almost immediately. We both did.

Sugar had found a quaint little club not far from the local military base, Fort Lee. She made a very good living doing… well…what Sugar does. I in turn, had found a receptionist job at Dr. Barnes Dentistry and was settling in quite nicely with this new uneventful life.

$ $ $

I was on my back, head facing north, eyes closed. My legs were trembling as they stood apart. I felt like I was floating as my current lover contined to lap at my insides, curled their tongue around my clitoris. Made my love button dance with the rhythm of tongue. How! I could only imagine, couldn't even fathom the skill it took to accomplish such a thing. But I enjoyed it, nonetheless.

"Oh God Azya," I exclaimed. "That's it…argh…that's my spot!"

Azya continued her oral assault on my sex. Never ceased her sinful manipulations for even a second. I attempted to close my legs with Azya trapped between them, squeezed her head in the process. I clutched at her hair as wave after blissful wave of smoldering orgasm wracked my body. It was so good, I wept. My tears fell from satisfaction, from the mental that accompanied the physical. Azya was an excellent lover, sporting a very talented tongue. It had taken some time to bring that out of her, but now she was my Frankenstein monster, my creation of sin. I just knew she would be a special one, when she came strolling through the office door and strutted her beautiful self up to my desk. We had each locked gazes with one another and the rest well…

I continued to benefit from this creation of mine. It's funny now that I think about things while basking in the afterglow of orgasm. I don't think, ever in her wildest imaginations, did Azya ever believe she would have a face full of pussy and love it. We had become inseparable over these last few weeks. I practically spent most, if not all of my free time, in her bed, cultivating this relationship.

Azya wasn't a free woman though. She was taken, belonged to another. That knowledge alone made me smile. The little vixen attempted to keep me in the dark about that minor detail when we started this affair. A fact I found rather amusing. She didn't understand that my homework had been done long before our so-called chance meeting and subsequent friendship. No, if she only knew what my true motivations, my real intentions were; she would have run.

I pushed her back, moved her off of me. "Let me up baby," I said.

Azya frowned, "I'm not finished with my snack just yet. I'm trying to make them pretty toes of yours to curl."

See what I mean, I have created a monster. "Gotta potty baby. Let me up," I stated. I got off the bed, ran to the bathroom; felt a little nauseous. Azya followed behind me...cautiously.

"What's wrong Ann?" She questioned.

"Nothing," I lied, was trying to answer her in between bouts of vomiting. Obviously, she knew I spoke an untruth. Azya came to my back then, worry and concern clearly etched on her face. She gently pulled my hair back from my face like she had performed this act many times before.

"Are you sure...you're—not"

"No! Fine... Azya...give it here," I said, cutting her off. "A little privacy please."

She stormed out. Left me alone then, somewhat reluctant. I read the instructions on the box she had handed me. Felt almost nervous as I did so. I thought over my possibilities here. Azya was a nice distraction but I knew this was just a temporary situation. I/we had business to attend to and that business would come calling very soon. Another bout of nausea hit me, had to kneel before the porcelain god once more. Had to be something I ate. Kept telling myself that, over and over.

As I knelt before the toilet, bringing forth today's

breakfast, back through my mouth and tastebuds; I overheard shouting and arguing off in the distance. It sounded like Azya was in a shouting match with some guy. That much I could make out from the tone of the other voice. Whoever it was, displayed that they were pissed the hell off at someone. I crept to the bathroom door, closed it till it was left slightly ajar, put my ear up to the door and easedropped as best I could.

"Just who in the hell were you fucking Azya!" The male voice shouted at the top of his lungs. "Our bed is a goddamn wreck, the room smells of sex and your damn skin is flushed like you been working out." He was good, I thought. "So... who the fuck have you been fucking...huh?"

"Nobody, Tony. I told you, I aint fucking nobody up in here... baby."

"Don't baby me bitch! I aint no damn fool. I been gone overseas fighting for us and I come back to this bullshit."

Bingo! It looks like the husband is back and this could either be a fun situation, or he coud complicate some shit for me and Azya.

I peeked into the bedroom to get a look at the cause of all the ruckus. Tony was a good looking man, was either a light skinned Black or a Latin brotha. It was hard to tell. He was of course in great shape and his body was to die for. I could see his muscles flexing through his tight tanktop and shorts, as his anger and rage continued to play out.

But just as sudden as the argument began, it ceased. He couldn't help but get aroused as he stood there fussing and staring at the beautiful half Black, half Chinese woman who was his wife; while she stood before him barely clothed. Azya was an exotic beauty. She had acquired the best of both races in the looks department. She displayed long silky black hair, slanted oval eyes that were light brown in color. She sported a tight but voluptuous frame, had curves to die for coupled with a very small waist. Azya had a 36DD chest partnered with a 35 inch ass, and she had no extra body fat. She was what some refer to as "slimthick" Basically, she was stacked from head to toe. I was almost jealous! Almost…

All that visual stimulation was just too much for poor old Tony to handle. After all, he was a young and virile man that had been away from his sexy bride for close to 6 months now. He straight up bum-rushed her, pulled her flesh revealing lacy top off. He threw her onto the unmade bed that I had just shared with her. I must admit, I was getting a little turned on watching him man handle that lovely ass. Tony was forceful with her, struck me as the type that likes to be totally dominant in the sack.

He jerked her to a position that had her on all fours, practically ripped her thong off, had her left leg up and was about to enter her from behind with one of the prettiest looking dicks I had ever seen. Damn! I wanted to wrap my lips around that wood the minute my eyes fell on it.

Azya almost screamed as he invaded her sex with little regard for mercy. She had been without that meat for 6 months now, it was the type of instrument that one had to keep servicing so your Eve could get use to accomadating such invasions. I knew he was stretching her wide, filling that snugness to capacity. I enjoyed it!

I continued to watch from my vantage point with growing lust and desires of my own. My nausea all but forgotten as I watched the two lovers before me, perform tantalizing sexual acts. Hell, it had been months for me as well. I longed to be filled and stroked the way Azya's male lover was sexing her.

Then I remembered what I held. I crept back to the bathroom to use it.

I heard," Oh—fuck! Yes baby...fuck this pussy! I'm your bitch!"

" You damn right! This is my pussy. Do you hear me goddammit! Who is beating this pussy up...huh, who?"

It was done. I walked slowly out of the bathroom toward the bedroom. I took a deep breath, entered the bedroom without being noticed initially. Azya saw me first. She pushed her husband away with much difficulty. I could tell she didn't want to break the connection of flesh.

"A-Ann?" She said, almost out of breath. "Baby, this is my friend Ann. She has been keeping me company while you have been gone. Been trying to take my mind off of missing you. She's been helping me with our daughter as well.

Tony stood. Naked. His Adam bobbed in all its magnificence. He held no shame, was proud of his unclothed display. I could tell he was taking in my assets as well. I saw approval in his eyes, saw lust there too. A smile crept over his face as his mind whirled. He saw possibilities.

"Azya," I said, rasing the small indicator. "I'm pregnant."

Look for Sugar's return in the upcoming novel:

Sugar-Free

Don't let his jump shot fool you. Once known locally for his basketball skills, Jo Dee Sanders began his literary career in his early 20's writing poetry and creating short stories for co-workers. His friends will tell you that rarely a day passes without him writing something—a thought, a statement, a story idea, a dialogue between characters yet unnamed. He continued to refine his craft through the years and now brings you a treat for your senses with his first major novel.

Jo Dee still resides in Durham, NC.

www.ingramcontent.com/pod-product-compliance
Lightning Source LLC
Chambersburg PA
CBHW061556170626
46811CB00001B/222